# EXTRA SENSE


## GINNY STROUD

# Prologue

How did I end up here?

In a five by ten Spartan room, where the only consolation is the air conditioning in an otherwise unbearably hot and unrelenting furnace.

I am from the northern hemisphere, so although the heat may be tolerable, the humidity is not.

This is the Deep South in July.

Its people are as warm as the temperature, but it is not a place I would choose to be at this season.

Neither would I be in this cell from choice.

For cell it is.

So why am I here?

In accommodation more likely to be found in the developing world, than one of its richest countries.

And one, I am certain, would not pass any health and safety regulations.

The bed is a sturdy metal contraption of torture, with, what could be more accurately be described as a bolster, than a mattress.

The pillow is thick, but again utilitarian.

It looks and feels like a sack of potatoes - I would rather not examine its contents!

The "assemble" is completed by a thin blanket, which has never seen the inside of a washing machine.

Again I would rather not enquire too deeply into its past, or present occupants!

But it does serve a dual purpose.

In daylight it does provide some protection against the aggressive air conditioning, and at night doubles as a shield against the "bugs."

In such climates night time brings a little relief from the

humidity, but also carries insects which are a nuisance at home, but are intolerable here.

Mosquitoes like flying vampire pterodactyls, who are hardened to cold and spray - if I had either.

For as soon as daylight fades, so apparently does the air conditioning!

Probably because most of the staff go home and electricity is an unwarranted luxury for prisoners.

I ask myself: doesn't this constitute cruel and unusual punishment?

As for insect repellent.

Well I did have some "Off" stashed away in my suitcase, but this is now confiscated and safely locked away.

No doubt in case I accidentally gassed myself as well as the "critters."

Finally, no accommodation is complete without bathroom facilities.

There is a toilet, again for security purposes, in full view.

But no seat - I would not risk sitting on it if there was.

A miniscule sink is somehow squeezed into a corner.

Though I have a firm conviction any ablutions would multiply rather than eliminate any germs.

My initial determination was to avoid both if my bodily functions would allow it.

I have been in here for almost 48 hours, so imagine how successful that was!

Sufficient it to say I am thankful to be the only occupant!!

All is now darkness apart from slivers cast by various items of technology in the nearby office.

Outside this thick walled and windowless gaol I know the night chorus is in full voice.

The tree frogs and crickets will occasionally be joined by their larger nocturnal companions, now most humans in this small town have gone to air conditioned earth.

I would join them in the arms of Morpheus but it is too hot to sleep and I have too much on my mind.

When I was a child I began keeping a diary and whether through dedication or superstition, have continued this practice.

It is still with me - in my quarantined suitcase!

But such lifetime habits are hard to break.

Those precautionary measures have again robbed me of the right to a pen or paper, but my mind is still free.

Freedom has its dangers and responsibilities, a fact many people advocating such rights seem to forget or ignore.

If I could not stop my thoughts I could direct them on a less hazardous route.

The past is much safer than the future.

It is known territory, although it is strewn with regrets and "what might have beens."

At the end of the day regrets are pointless and what is done is done.

The past may be less exciting but it is so much more secure than the future.

The only certainty about the future is at some point, sooner or later, death will be waiting for you.

On our individual roads, there may be a choice of routes, but there are no off ramps, no toll roads, only dead ends!

And therein lies my problem - my gift or curse - which has put me in this prison.

With my experience of life I know it does not end with death any more than it begins with conception.

So where did this all begin for me?

Well I suppose, if I had to pick a moment, it would be almost sixty years ago.

A moment in the past when the earth seemed to revolve at a slower pace and there was time to spare.

Somewhere in this new technological "wonderland" humanity seems to have lost its sense of personal accountability.

In doing so we have exorcised our guilt, but we have also thrown out a great deal of our capacity for imagination and compassion.

Children are born free, but everywhere find themselves chained within their own little bubbles.

It is a beguilingly sheltered existence, but it is not living.

Life is about uncertainty and emotion: neither of which are always comfortable feelings.
But pleasure and pain are what make you human, make you alive.
Keep you truly free.

My physical body may be imprisoned within this cell, but my thoughts are still my own.
So I liberate them to travel back over the decades to a different time, and, in my perhaps biased mind, a better place.

# Chapter One: Born

With the help of my mental time machine, the original modified DeLorean, I am back in 1950.

In the words of a far, far better author - "I am born."

I was born on the Sabbath day - although I cannot say I was always blithe and bonny.

Certainly not good or gay - in either sense of the word!

A chubby Churchillian baby, newly delivered at home to a mother who will never really know me, but a grandmother who has never really left me.

Later she would share the memory of our introduction.

It was a time when childbirth was still fraught with danger for both mother and child.

I can imagine my grandmother's relief when the midwife appeared to announce both were well and healthy.

She remembers as she entered the bedroom my head turned and our eyes met.

She says they were bright blue, although sadly they have never been since!

Apparently the nurse said I had opened my eyes just before my mother pushed and I squirmed my way out into this world.

So, as a new born not only was I as yet incapable of 50/50 vision, but I was under the disadvantage of a very unpleasant eye wash.

Nevertheless for her it always remained a sweet moment, a treasured memory.

And, with the luxury of hindsight, extremely prophetic.

Time and recollection move on, as they always must.

Not very far, because just ten months later, I was legally adopted by my maternal grandparents.

Of course I don't remember any of this, but I later learnt of my parents' divorce.

After which they both went their separate ways.

Neither in my direction.

A fact for which I soon learnt to be everlastingly grateful.

In exchange for a future, which would be tainted by the fallout from marital trouble and strife, I had loving and wise grandparents.

In an age where divorce was still a source of stigma they did an amazing job of giving their granddaughter a sense of her own value.

Any social difference was quickly transformed into a reason for feeling special.

So I grew up as normal as any other baby boomer of the 1950s could.

Perhaps a lot better than many of my friends!

All our childhood, and later teenage years, was lived under the very real threat of extinction courtesy of a nuclear bomb.

My grandparents, who had had their own "sword of Damocles" hanging over their heads in the form of the Blitz, adopted their usual sensible approach.

"What cannot be changed must be borne."

So while I don't think The Cold War ruined my formative years, it could not help but shape them.

But you cannot live in a state of perpetual fear for long before the mind revolts - one way or another.

Perhaps this is exactly what happened to my generation during the Rebellious Fifties and the Swinging Sixties!

Most infections reach a crisis point: fear is not a virus but it is both dangerous and highly contagious.

For us I believe it reached this turning point in 1962 in an event thousands of miles away.

A confrontation between the superpowers aptly known as "The Cuban Missile Crisis."

It is an early memory so powerful that to this day I can revisit and feel those emotions.

I was eleven years old, sitting a classroom with my friends, where, I can guarantee, none of us remember the lesson or teacher.

It was quiet, but not through concentration.

More like the eerie silence in church during prayer.

Not far from the truth, because my silent request was to see my grandparents once more.

Of course at eleven years old I didn't know anything about the political implications.

All I knew was that two far away countries: America and Russia were probably about to blow up our planet and destroy us all over some childish adult squabble.

I was scared, but I was also very very angry.

An anger I had never known before because it was not my well known hot blooded temper.

Instead it was a cold numbing sensation where thought and movement seemed impossible.

As an adult I understand now this was probably the result of pent up emotion with no obvious outlet.

The primitive "fight or flight response" when neither action is available.

All I do remember was the thought "if I am going to die I want to be with the people I love and love me."

As history now records - those prayers were answered.

Because, although I felt alone, I now know that it was a time when most of humanity held its breath.

The crisis had passed, but such traumatic events always leave something behind.

As far as I was concerned this was the determination never to take my loved ones for granted, and never to live in fear again.

Probably a perfect mantra for the 1960s and 70s.

So I grew up, in more ways than one, during that momentous era.

Sex, drugs and rock and roll.

Well not for me free love (and for love read sex) or escape into the psychedelic haze of LSD or magic mushrooms.

Even a Marijuana spliff was unlikely to pass lips which had never held a cigarette.

There is a saying "if you remember the 60s you weren't really there."

But this was coined in the 70s by people who really, to all intents and purposes, were not there and were only just coming round from the experience.

Well I was there and remember.

I remember the multitude of pop, if not rock, groups whose genuine talent temporarily obscured such extraordinary genius as The Beatles.

I remember, in my later teens, outings with friends into cities which are now so dangerous they have become virtual "no go" areas.

I remember it was a time of innocence but it was also an awakening about our responsibility to the planet.

I see this is a fact almost forgotten now.

There is a new generation, who believe they have all the answers, and can learn nothing from the mistakes and successes of the past.

It is perhaps no accident two of the largest environmental organisations: the WWF (1961) Greenpeace (1971)were formed at that time.

Every generation, with the energy and arrogance of youth, believes they are the first.

The first to recognise the problem, the first to care, the first to try to make a difference!

I wish them luck because they have yet to learn the sad truth: people who forget their past have no future.

And the past tells us that change always requires great personal sacrifice.

In this materialistic age I am not sure anyone is prepared for that!

I also remember this was the time my "problems" really began and nothing afterwards was ever quite the same.

# Chapter Two:  Special


In order for you to understand this I need to go back and explain this event was just another natural progression.

The whole thing should hardly have been surprising since my genes contained those of  my grandmother and the grandmother before her.

The only thing surprising about it was my existence at all.

How a long line of "witches" had survived the trials and persecutions of the past.

This is not to infer my beloved grandmother was indeed a "witch" in any magical (black or white) sense of the word.

As far as I know she didn't belong to a coven,  cast any spells, or, more usefully,  concoct any potions.

She was just "special."

She had an acute sensitivity to her surroundings and the people within it.

I am convinced most babies are born with this natural ability.

But as society begins to take over their development such childish things are put away.

Or, are so repressed they may as well no longer exist.

But they are still there under the veneer of conformity placed upon us.

Only beneath the surface in my case as nature and nurture came together in the form of my grandmother.

So although, try as I might,  this "gift" has never successfully been put away in a cupboard and forgotten.

This may be part of my grandmother's legacy, but I cannot accuse her of any undue influence or encouragement.

Yes I remember the ghost stories she recounted.

Not the usual second hand folklores,  but personal remembered narratives.

All of them gave me a creepy pleasure, but none of them left me with anything but the determination I never wanted to experience them first hand.

I think she understood this because such sessions always ended with the disclaimer: "of course it's all a load of rubbish."

Not totally convincing since one of the stories in particular had all the factual requirements of the truth.

One which I knew as "The Ghostly Horseman."

It concerned the early history of my grandparents romance and a motorcycle ride they often made to visit relatives near Stratford upon Avon.

On this particular occasion the journey was made late at night - the witching hour.

Midnight: the death of one day and the birth of another: when ghosts walk the earth - or in this case - ride.

The tale goes that they were riding along the old A34 from Oxford to Stratford when they were suddenly joined by another traveller.

A horseman was galloping alongside them, whose steed must have been winged Pegasus as it kept pace with their own trusty Triumph.

The unexpected event apparently led to a few rare expletives from my normally quiet and gentle grandfather.

But the apparition, for there was no other explanation, suddenly was no longer there.

A development which caused the couple to stop the bike and look around.

It was the middle of the night, but there was a full moon and no hedgerows to provide cover.

Nowhere to hide the man - let alone his large companion.

Of course the tale always ended with the usual dismissal.

But it is very hard to erase what has been so eloquently imprinted, particularly when I knew full well my grandmother was no liar.

My apologies for my own lengthy retelling of this tale, but it does have a purpose, along with, I hope, some entertainment value.

Many years later I discovered the validation for this story in a local guide book.

Apparently in the 18th century a farmer, worse for drink, was riding back from his local inn, knocked from his horse by a low branch and killed.

Legend has it that his spectre is seen replaying his final ride along this stretch of road near Atherstone.

Cynics would dismiss the whole story as superstitious twaddle. The more scientific and liberal critics would cite the well known "stone tape theory."

A phenomena when traumatic incidents in the past are so strongly reprinted on their surroundings that they are replayed, over and over like a tape recording.

In this instance such could well be the explanation, except for one thing.

My grandmother swore that as the apparition drew alongside he turned his head and looked directly at her.

He was as aware of her existence as she was of his!

As I said my grandmother was no liar.


The point of this narrative is simple: this was the reality of my childhood.

If it had just been the occasional ghost story then I could have easily forgotten it.

But I could not because I knew it was all true.

I knew, not because I had seen any phantoms, but because of my own unusual and unwanted experiences.

They - whomever they may be - say such things skip a generation.

This was certainly the case in our family.

As far as I could tell my mother had no such natural abilities, or disabilities, and I think I would have known since she desperately wanted them.

No, without being harsh, my biological mother had the alleged insensitivity of a fish.

On the other hand as I grew up not only did my sixth sense - for want of a better word - not diminish it became stronger.

My first memories of such events manifested themselves as instances of instant aversion to people and places.

Places came first.

Old buildings and locations with a long and varied human occupation were a particularly rich source.

Most of the time such feelings were fascinating rather than frightening.

I remember once, on one of the trips to London with my grandfather, visiting the Tower.

He had left me for a few minutes - no doubt to answer a call of nature .

He knew I was safe - the courtyard was empty apart from a couple of distant yeoman warders.

I had been well briefed in the warning "never take sweets" and certainly never "go off" with strangers.

Although this advice did seem at odds with the acceptance of some oddly dressed man slipping down our chimney once a year to deliver presents!

Besides I was older now and completely disillusioned about Father Christmas.

It was winter,  out of season,  even the ravens were sheltering and quiet.

But for me the place was alive.

Oh there were no apparitions,  headless or otherwise, even though I was sitting close to the chapel and execution site.

It was feeling rather than sight which convinced me I was not alone.

It only lasted for a few moments,  until my grandfather returned, but it was not unpleasant.

However,  as I grew up,  I discovered such experiences are not always so welcome.

Once in particular,   on another outing,  this time with my mother,  I remember being taken to a friend's house.

At that time my mother had married an American airman and was living on base.

It was just standard military housing:  a two up, two down semi detached, with a small useful yard.

Nothing distinguished it from its uniform neighbours.

But it repelled me.

I remember looking at my mother as we approached: there was

no reaction.

But then, as I said, she had virtually no sensitivity.

The closer we got to the front door the more I was certain of one fact about the future: I would not be going through it.

I knew my mother would not understand - to her I was already a strange, alien creature.

I possessed not one of her traits, not one of her values.

Hardly surprising since I had probably only been in her company a few weeks since my birth.

You cannot bond with a stranger, even if you have spent the first nine months together!!

So I made some excuse - I cannot remember what.

The strategy wasn't important, the result was.

And it was a success.

I spent the entire visit outside in the garden, which fortunately could be accessed via a back gate.

Not something which endeared me to my mother, but on the other hand she was probably equally grateful.

Over the years I never knew her to show any pride in me, or later, my accomplishments.

In fact she never claimed any hand, or indeed any other part of her anatomy, in my existence.

Indeed as a young child she had warned me I had been sent by the Devil and one day he would take me back!

Of course always out of my grandparents' earshot.

She might be insensitive but she was not stupid.

After her return from a failed romance in America she did try to remould me in her image.

Too little, too late: it was already set.

Thereafter she made no effort to disguise her disapproval.

So instead she resorted to criticism of my character and behaviour.

This incident would be yet another weapon in her arsenal.

Thankfully she was not around long.

America in the form of the United States Air Force beckoned once more.

Anyway, not to make a long story any longer, as with the

"ghostly horsemen," there is a point to this story.

This came much later when I was grown up.

My mother now lived in America, with two new children, whom thank goodness she appeared to truly love.

She was on one of her annual pilgrimages home, and I chauffeured her around to visit old friends.

One of these was the lady from base housing which had so unsettled me years earlier.

Thankfully there was no such problem with her new home near Bath.

After retirement she and her G.I. husband had retired back to the UK.

She was a native of that county and so we were treated to a traditional "high" tea with crustless cucumber sandwiches and the local delicacy Bath buns.

Before we left the conversation came around to their time in the Air Force.

Although I had only been half listening, when the topic changed to "the house" I could literally feel my ears prick up.

It was a warm and sunny day.

Sylvia, for that was her name, had an equally bright and bubbly personality.

But suddenly my memories were back when I was standing outside that awful place.

It turned out I had good reason.

Apparently the house had a bad history, which Sylvia herself only found out later.

I contributed nothing to the conversation, and my mother seemed to have forgotten my odd behaviour, but what I heard was enough.

It turned out it had been the scene of gruesome double murder and suicide.

A previous tenant, during its military occupation, had arrived home from an overseas posting.

From which he was so traumatized he had taken a gun and blown away his wife, child and self.

I was shocked but not surprised.

Because by this time I had changed.

I had learnt to trust, if not appreciate, my gut feelings.

But what had changed me was not my receptiveness to places, it was people.

This was triggered by an incident in my late teens when I learnt how valuable, if not vital, was this instinct.

And while it could be a curse, it was also a blessing - which should never, ever, be disregarded or questioned.

A dislike of certain places may be unsettling and inconvenient, but ignoring an aversion to people could prove to be dangerous.

I almost found that out one evening with my closest friend Linda.

We had been invited to a birthday party at a mutual friend's home.

An innocent enough undertaking.

All went well, we even met two young men, who could be described as "personable," or that most damning of descriptions "nice."

But my psychic antenna started vibrating: there was something about them it did not like.

So when the party started to peter out, and we were offered a lift home, I wanted to do anything but get in their car.

Peer pressure, combined with a fear of irrational rudeness, overrode all the advice and warnings drummed into me from childhood.

Besides Linda was determined to accept the offer: she probably liked her "partner" more than I cared for mine!

It never occurred to me to let her go alone.

Because I had remembered another well repeated mantra "safety in numbers."

I actually found myself getting into a car with "strangers."

There was no excuse: we could easily have walked the half a mile home.

Of course there was never any intention to go straight home, and we soon found ourselves driving down some local dark lane.

I was sitting in the front seat and was dismayed to see the driver park and turn off the engine.

Not an unexpected event, in fact with teenagers almost a rite of passage.

But to me it was like watching a nightmare start to unfold.

In the darkness I could hear activity on the back seat, and for the first time that evening I acted on pure instinct rather than social convention.

I flung open my door and just stood there shouting for Linda to get out and come with me.

The shock, either from the unexpected tone of my voice, or the sudden recollection of all the lectures instilled into us, sent her flying out of the car.

I don't know whether we mumbled any apologies or explanations to our companions, but we took off back up the dark, thankfully, short lane.

I do remember neither of us spoke a word until we reached our homes and that we never discussed it again.

There was no need, it was a lesson learnt.

It may have ended there, except it was reinforced a few weeks later.

Imagine my surprise when my grandmother commented on an article in the headlines of the local newspaper.

Two young girls had been raped, beaten and left for dead.

Fortunately an off duty village Bobbie had witnessed the attack before murder had been committed.

He recognised the two youths, whom had run off, but been arrested and charged within forty eight hours.

She probably wouldn't have been so shocked except the crime had taken place in a nearby village.

I probably wouldn't have paid much attention except the images of two seemingly "nice" boys was also spread across the front page.

I hardly need to tell you it was our "escorts" from the birthday party!

I don't know if Linda ever found out about this terrible sequel to our night out.

As I said we never discussed it again.

But for me it was the moment I could no longer ignore the curse, or blessing, I had inherited.

It was the moment I grew up.

At the end of the day also the reason I have ended up in this cell.

# Chapter Three: Growing

It is almost dawn now.
I can tell by the wall clock in the office.
Its face is not completely visible to me, except the little hand
which is just past three.
I have barely slept.
Just cat naps leaning against the hard, but cool and clean, stone
wall.
How the time passes when you are having fun.
Well for the most part my memories are happy ones.
But into everyone's life some rain must fall, and if it doesn't
then you are probably not living.
There's one consolation, whatever happens now, I did have a
life.
A quote from a film comes to mind.
Cleopatra, I believe, because it is Richard Burton as Mark
Anthony who says : "You know, Octavian... it's possible that
when you die, you will die without ever having been alive."
Well I am still alive and once again slip back into the safe world
of the past.
Which is not to say it is always a happy land filled with joyful
memories.
They say trouble always comes in threes.
In the same year I was understanding the real value of my 'gift'
there was at least one other unforgettable event.
Perhaps there was a third, now obscured over the passage of
time.
In fact it was the first incident, since it happened in March
before the fateful birthday party.
But was so sudden and traumatic that, for me, it temporarily
eclipsed everything else.
It was the death of my quiet and gentle grandfather.
He was only fifty eight years old, and although we realised with
hindsight the significance of his increasingly frequent
headaches, otherwise he seemed fit and well.

He did not have - or did not know he had - any of the usual middle aged ailments.

No diabetes, not even blood pressure warnings.

But one morning he went out to dig our elderly neighbour's garden and never returned.

He died from a massive coronary thrombosis.

When a small and seemingly innocuous blood clot stopped his large and generous heart.

Apparently his body was lifeless before it hit the ground.

The medics later consoled us with the fact that if there had been pain he did not feel it for long.

There really was no consolation.

He was a good man, a "gentle" man in the best sense of the word.

The timelessness of grief asking the same old question.

Why should he be taken when there were much more worthy candidates?

It didn't make sense and it wasn't fair.

Neither mine, nor my grandmother's faith, seemed to help very much in those dark days and darker nights.

What I do remember was the overwhelming sense of finality.

We would never to be able to see or speak to my beloved grandfather again.

But I was wrong, and by the time my grandmother rejoined him twenty five years later, I knew it.

For now though I go back to those grim days which would change me forever.

Death always does, and not only for the deceased!

I would eventually come to terms with his loss, but I would never again feel any certainty about the future.

It may offer many wonderful possibilities, but it is also the great unknown.

If we are wise we accept what we cannot control and make the most of what we have.

Of course my grandmother knew all this, but for the moment she was heartbroken and overwhelmed by loss.

I am not sure you ever really recover from such grief.

Time, the supposed great healer, only really numbs the pain, it is always there under the surface.

When my grandfather died his most personal, and therefore precious possessions, were handed to me.

The one item of real monetary value, the gold watch presented to him after 25 years' service at the Rover factory, was given to my young brother.

I did not care about it, any more than he had.

I don't think he ever even tried it on!

Instead I kept, and treasured, the few things he had in his pockets.

A veritable trove.

An old battered steel watch, a few coins, a lighter, and most poignant of all, a packet of cigarettes, which contained his last half smoked stub.

It broke my heart when I saw this collection of "worthless" things, so I buried them away.

On the rare occasions when they are unearthed it still does.

No, time does not heal.

# Chapter Four: Pains

But soon, after the ordeal of the funeral, my grandmother and I slowly began to recover.

My mother and siblings returned to their life, at that time on a USAF base in Germany.

We were left to build a new life together: a smaller but, in some ways, a much closer unit.

At first daily life carried on much as normal.

What my grandfather had lacked in formal education, was more than compensated in common sense.

He had taken out an insurance policy against the mortgage so the house was now our home.

Financially, thanks to the State pension, and a large company lump sum, we were reasonably well off.

Besides in those pre technology days there was little to spend money on!

My grandmother did her best, and succeeded, in shielding me from much of the daily household concerns.

She continued to clean, cook and pay bills.

I continued to work.

Ironically in the secretarial training school, a new post my grandfather had secured for me at the Rover plant.

It was always a source of great regret that my acceptance letter arrived a week after his death.

At the time, and for a long time to come, I was frustrated and angry that I could no longer thank him.

Other jobs we shared.

She loved her garden and I enjoyed redecorating, which in the age of "flower power" often meant the most garish wallpapers available.

But she tolerated it all, with maybe a humorous comment, never a complaint.

So life went on.

The cold war had cooled down and although the threat was still there we had learnt to live with it.

Like a very large, but familiar, elephant in the room.
Besides there seemed to be so much more going on in the world.
The swinging sixties had passed and many people had woken up in the seventies.
It was a time of numerous conflicts, headed by the continuance of The Vietnam War and beginning of the Northern Ireland "troubles."
Yet for every action there is always a reaction, and this spawned the "peace" movement.
There was also a growing realisation about the fragile nature of our Earth and our responsibility to it.
We, the younger generation, were the ones going to solve all the problems and save the planet.
Ah the conceit of youth again!
Good intentions, but we all know where that particular road is said to lead.
Unfortunately, more often it's a case of the world changing us than the other way round.
As for me, well as the decade progressed, so did I.
I grew older and wiser.
Despite the saying, I have discovered many people do not actually learn anything by either age or experience.
Perhaps my development was due to the necessity of circumstance.
As the years passed my grandmother's strength, and therefore physical abilities, began to diminish.
She continued to keep the house clean and produce the tasty substantial meals she had cooked since her days in domestic service.
But every year I took over more of the heavier maintenance work and managed all financial matters.
My wages had increased enough for me to be regarded as "the bread winner."
My grandmother's pension was her own, although she spent most of it on groceries and me!
Habits of a lifetime are hard to break.

So by my mid twenties I had acquired a maturity beyond my years.

A sense of responsibility, I came to learn, many adults successfully avoid all their lives.

I am sorry if this seems an irrelevant, and so no doubt boring, narrative of my life.

But like my earlier diversions it does serve a purpose in this story.

If I describe this time as ordinary, then perhaps in one way it was.

I was growing up and, like everyone else, was trying to find my place in a society I had not helped create.

I was growing up and, with the naivety of youth, believed I could change the world, or at least reshape it a little.

Make a difference.

It was an exciting time when all things appeared possible, before we learnt the truth,

We do not live in the best of all possible worlds.

We live in an imperfect world where democracy and freedom of speech are much discussed, but seldom seen.

Human beings are flawed:   their personal egos stronger than the survival of their own kind.

What chance for so called lesser species?

Or to put it simply.

Whatever they may say - no one really wants to be equal.

All this I had yet to learn.

So I was finding my way, believing it was a previously untrodden path - like everyone else.

In another way I was completely unlike anyone else, but it was not a distinction I cared to advertise.

Besides since the episode of the birthday party there had been no further evidence.

# Chapter Five: Sense

This is not to say I had suddenly lost all my highly tuned sensitivities.

Rather the case such feelings were something I had become used to.

Places which made me happy or sad.

People I did like and people I did not.

The latter impulse seemed so unfair, that for years I fought against it.

I argued that any prejudice against a new acquaintance was completely irrational.

And I handled the problem by overcompensation.

But this had a strange outcome.

The more I struggled for their friendship the stronger became my aversion.

Like a small insistent voice telling me to listen.

So eventually I gave up fighting.

I still tried to find the best in people, and still do, but I soon abandoned my "benefit of the doubt" strategy.

Too many times this had been seen as a weakness to exploit, and used against me.

It never ceased to amaze me that none of them appeared to see through, what I thought, a flimsy mask.

They were either too absorbed in themselves, or I was a better actor than I thought!

There were some, probably with more intuition than the rest, who looked uncomfortable around me.

And a few who avoided me like the plague.

In any case as I grew older I came to accept my first impressions were always right.

So I reached a sort of impasse.

Whenever I felt my personal alarm vibrating, I tried not to wear on my face what I felt in my heart.

But I never ignored the warning.

I had finally come to trust my instincts.

At around this time I became aware of another, for want of a better word, "quirk," which would have been extremely useful, if I could have controlled it!

This manifested itself in the ability to know the answers to impossible questions .

For example, someone would ask me "you'll never guess what football team so and so supports."

It would have to be a guess because I couldn't possibly know - but I always did!

A useful gift at last.

One which could have made me rich, except for one fact.

The only time it worked was when I wasn't thinking.

I would just know into which slot a roulette ball would fall when the answer came from my mouth without passing my brain.

The moment thought entered the equation all was lost.

If you think there is an easy solution - try emptying the space between your own ears.

Of course other people noticed this strange phenomenon - even tried to use it.

In the end, when I couldn't perform to order, they concluded it was some sort of trick.

In a way it was.

But the secret was not in a sleight of hand, it was being in the right state of mind.

Or rather no state of mind: a sort of trance.

Perhaps I should have teamed up with a hypnotist.

We could have made a fortune.

Except, somehow I always felt if I didn't use this "gift" I should never misuse it.

As I said earlier all power carries responsibility or should.

This was all well and good, but very soon I would receive another insight into my "condition" which would change everything.

Up until that moment I thought I knew my limitations.

Afterwards I didn't know their perimeters, or indeed if any existed.

I cannot remember a time when I could not pick up feelings

from places and people.

As a child I had accepted my grandmother's ghost stories as gospel, not just because I loved her deeply, but because I knew they were true.

In my late teens I had asked her why she was so certain about the outcome of future events.

An ability for which many family and friends jokingly labelled her a witch.

She explained she just knew when everything would be all right - and it always was.

I accepted this because what had prompted this question were my own first hand experiences.

Not often, but in rare moments of overwhelming panic.

It came as a strange, light headed sensation, which took away all fear: leaving behind only the certainty "all is right with the world."

My first remembered acquaintance with this had been while sitting in a classroom aged eleven waiting to die.

An encounter I had chosen to dismiss and forget under the excuse of extreme stress.

In any event, I never wanted to believe any other possible explanation.

I preferred to put such peculiarities down to coincidence, or my overly receptive emotional antenna.

For what was to happen next, I can give no rational explanation, offer no logical argument.

# Chapter Six:  Sensitivity

As Shakespeare says through Hamlet:  "there are more things in Heaven and Earth,  Horatio,  than are dreamt of in your philosophy."

One of these things, for me, took place at the beginning of another decade.

It was the middle of March 1980 and I was having a drink with an old school friend in a local pub.

There was absolutely nothing as welcoming from the outside, or as comforting on the inside,  as a traditional inn on a cold dark evening.

Sadly nowadays they seem to be a dying breed, having been replaced by the wine bar, or dreaded gastro pub.

A modern innovation where the décor is usually as inviting as a hospital waiting room and the price list requires an estimate.

Fortunately you can usually distinguish these establishments by the trendy sepia sign suspended outside!

I may be doing these places an injustice,  but in my limited experience,  they are living proof not all progress is an improvement!

But in March 1980 such developments were,  thankfully, a thing of the future.

The weather was normal for that month - being completely abnormal.

March had come in as a lamb,  in fact it had been unseasonably mild,

This evening though the winds were getting up, and the temperatures were going down.

Indeed the Met Office forecast some sleet for the end of the week.

All the signs indicated it would be going out like a lion.

The landlord had earlier lit a fire, which was now blazing and crackling in the ancient hearth.

We had grabbed two nearby armchairs,  where we were enjoying a couple of after dinner brandies.

We had dined early, so now most of the patrons had moved into the restaurant.

The "snug" where we sat was almost empty - except for a couple, who were obviously more interested in each other than food.

As we sat in that blissful contented state, when bodily comforts have been satisfied, talk turned to holidays.

Probably a natural progression given the current weather.

Joan, my friend, told me she was planning an escape to the sun in April.

She was due time off from her job, and was looking, as many people did then and ever since, at Spain.

We finished the conversation, and our drinks, then reluctantly headed out into the weather.

We said goodbye in the car park, with a pledge to catch up again soon, before getting into our respective taxis.

For once such a promise was kept.

One evening, just two days later, Joan rang me.

The main reason being to thank me for suggesting such a lovely evening.

But before she rang off she told me "oh by the way I booked that break - not Spain - I got a deal on a flight to Tenerife"

I have to say at the time I don't remember any reaction to this news.

For me, overseas holidays were limited to visiting my family across The Pond, I probably didn't even know where Tenerife was.

I was soon to find out.

That night the dreams began.

Oh I know everyone has dreams, whether they remember them or not.

More rare are those visions so powerful and clear they stay with you after waking.

Those which either continue once you drift off again, or keep you awake.

I've had a few of these myself.

Exhausting, stressful, but previously none which made any

sense.

This time was different.

Since dreams had never played any part in my strange experiences, in the cold light of day I tried to find a rational explanation.

Joan, her holiday, the plane, all had featured in the dream, but these had also formed part of our late night telephone conversation.

Easy to dismiss as the subconscious replaying reality.

It took another twenty four hours for the dream to become a nightmare.

When I went to bed the next night , I can honestly say, both the telephone conversation and dream had been forgotten.

It had been a busy day, new events had eclipsed the old, and I was exhausted.

As soon as my head hit the pillow I fell into a deep sleep.

I don't know how soon afterwards the dreams began.

Once more Joan was there.

But this time it was not a series of disjointed snapshots it was a movie.

The plane was also there and this time I saw her getting on it.

It should have been a happy moment,

She was exchanging smiles with a stewardess - anticipating a wonderful holiday.

But instead, as I watched the plane take off, I had an increasing sense of panic.

That's when it became a nightmare.

All the ingredients: trying to shout without a sound, trying to run without being able to move.

Overwhelmed and helpless.

So I did the one thing you can do in dreams you cannot do in reality - I woke myself up.

After a few moments, and a lot of deep breathing, I calmed down enough to fall back to sleep.

Almost as soon as my eyes closed, within what seemed like seconds, I was back at the airport watching that plane climb higher.

I woke myself up three more times that night - while each time the plane reached a little further into the sky.

Whatever happened I was determined not to see it disappear completely.

Like the old adage, if you dream you are falling, and you hit the bottom, you will die.

Although who has lived to tell the truth of this tale!

I finally found peaceful sleep at around 3am.

Fortunately it was a Sunday morning so I slept in.

Later on, when my grandmother commented on my restless night, I began to explain with the words "bad dream."

She stopped me dead with one of her favourite sayings:
"Saturday night's dream on a Sunday told is sure to come true before a month old."

I never described my dream to anyone that Sunday - or afterwards - until now.

Again I have my reasons.

But I did go over the details in my head, and found a new piece of information, which bothered me.

Somewhere I clearly remembered the words "Manchester airport."

This made no sense whatsoever: I had never been to Manchester let alone the airport, so why would my brain include this in any dream?

It bothered me so much I made a decision.

I waited until Monday morning - not taunting superstition or tempting fate - to ring Joan.

Luckily there was no repeat performance on Sunday night.

I had plenty of time to think this out, so I simply asked her if she needed a lift to Heathrow - our nearest airport.

She replied: no she would be fine.

In any case she was flying from Manchester so she was taking a coach a few days before to visit friends.

I cannot say my blood ran cold, but it certainly chilled down a little!

Her innocent little answer had raised more questions.

Where did I go from here?

What, if anything, do I do about this?

And on and on.

By Tuesday morning I knew all the answers and had only one question.

How could I stop her taking that flight?

Because on Monday night my nightmares resumed.

The film had rewound and was back at the airport: it was Manchester.

I could clearly see a sign at the entrance.

As before Joan boarded the plane, and smiled at the stewardess.

Cut to plane taking off.

This time though I didn't cover my eyes or turn away.

Every emotion told me to stop - to wake up, but I knew I should not.

However awful this was it was sent to me for a reason.

So I fought the impulse and carried on watching as the plane disappeared into the clouds.

As a distraction I tried to memorise every small detail.

Even in my dream state I was rational enough to feel this was important.

The screen went black.

Nothing happened for what seemed like several minutes, but was probably a few seconds.

Then I heard a sound.

At first I couldn't understand what it was and then my memory recalled a cold night in a pub.

A fire, not like a small hearth blaze, or even a bonfire, but a real conflagration.

It became louder - overpowering.

And still the screen remained black - which made it so much worse.

Story tellers and film makers learnt years ago the power of darkness to stimulate the imagination and paralyse the human mind with terror.

Just when I felt I could stand it no longer I woke up.

It was Tuesday morning - the bedside clock told me it was 1.21 am.

No more sleep - I had a question to answer "How could I stop Joan getting on that plane?"
I could have an early night later.
I knew somehow I would never have to watch this particular film again: its job was done.
I was right - I slept like a baby.
If any more dreams came it would not be that one.
But I still had a little under a month to come up with something.
Funnily enough I never queried the truth of my premonition.
Because I was certain that's exactly what it was.
OK I may be wrong - I may look a fool and lose a friend.
But what if I wasn't.
Then people would look at me with fear rather than ridicule, and my friend would lose her life.
How could I live with that?
So for the next two weeks I went through all possible options - including some minor assault on my friend requiring hospitalisation!
I was that desperate - that sure.
For every solution there seemed to be a dozen objections.
My first thought was to contact the airline.
I knew which one.
The final dream had shown it clearly written along the fuselage of the plane.
That was quickly ruled out.
Who would believe me?
I may even end up in prison for terrorism, or in a psychiatric hospital for evaluation.
Helplessly waiting for the newspapers which would either vindicate me as a freak, or confirm my guilt.
Neither with a very desirable outcome.
Either way my friend would be dead.
Strangely enough during all this time I only once considered all the other passengers and crew of that flight.
It wasn't all those innocent souls didn't matter to me, but I saw no practical way to help them.
I suppose I could stand at the airport on 25th April waving a

placard and shouting warnings, which doesn't come under the category "practical."

Back to the cell or straitjacket scenario!

Besides I had a difficult enough task trying to save my friend.

So what was I to do?

In the end I opted for the obvious.

Honesty is not always the most comfortable choice, but it is often the best policy.

So, after wasting two weeks searching for a viable alternative, I simply decided to tell her the truth.

Although I cannot say it is was an easy decision, and was anything but simple.

I was relying almost completely on our long friendship.

I say "almost" because I have found there is still a little superstition left in all of us.

Some primitive belief left over from the days before science tried to provide a theory for everything, and never quite succeeded.

So this was my plan.

Even though she had known me for years, she could well conclude I had suddenly lost my marbles.

The only thing left would be the conflict between some ancient illogical feeling and practical commonsense.

In which case she would probably ignore me and get on that plane.

It was a risky strategy, but it was the only one I had: there was no back up plan.

So I rang her and suggested we get together once more before her holiday.

The same pub was suggested for the next week.

Just four days before she left for the North.

Time was running out.

We met up as before and once more went straight into the dining room.

Again afterwards we found two comfortable seats by the still blazing fire.

If you believed in such things it was déjà vu - I was praying

Joan did!

We sat sipping our brandies.

Joan happy and relaxed, while I was, quite literally, summing up the bottle to destroy this.

We were on our second brandies before my Dutch courage was up to the task.

I took a deep breath and began.

I am not sure exactly what I said, or even how I started the conversation.

Although I don't recall Joan actually saying very much.

To be fair, what could she say?

I know I tried to speak slowly and sound rational, but when I ended my speech I didn't feel I had even convinced myself.

Joan never said a word while we finished our drinks and left the pub.

I have endured many uncomfortable silences since, but never so stony.

Never so terrible.

I had not only failed, I had lost (in more ways than one) a dear friend.

I wanted to say something more, not to end like this, but I knew it would only make matters worst.

The best I could hope was Joan would continue to think about what I had said even if she never spoke to me again.

Then it would be worth it.

When the taxis came we entered them without a word.

Hers began to pull away first - then stopped.

She rolled her window down and asked "Do you believe all this?"

I just looked at her and nodded.

She returned my gesture, and gave me a brief sad smile.

I have never seen her since.

At 1.21 pm a week later a plane crashed on Tenerife, there were no survivors.

A day afterwards I received a telephone call from a familiar voice which broke my heart because I knew I would probably never hear it again.

There was no conversation, just two words, "Thank You."
Of course I understood completely why Joan has not been in touch.
Why our friendship ended.
Who wants to be with someone who may be able to read your thoughts and predict your future?
No point in telling her I could do neither - it was just a one off blessing - or burden.
Perhaps, like myself, she was feeling some sort of guilt.
I told you earlier I didn't give much consideration to all those other passengers and crew before the disaster.
I didn't know them personally.
I have never sought any details.
I have never seen any accusing apparitions.
But I have never forgotten them.
I have never stopped asking myself: "why?"
I imagine it's a question Joan also asks.

But this experience served another purpose, it made me really stop and think about my meaning in life.
All those peculiarities, which I had inherited but so far managed to ignore.
All those responsibilities I was given but somehow managed to avoid.
All this I was suddenly forced to accept and understand: along with the strengths and weaknesses.
Yes, I saved a life, but why not all?
I had no answer - it seemed a useless two edged sword if I could not direct it.
It just felt so arbitrary - so random.
I imagine some people may enjoy feeling rudderless, I was not one of them.
But in the end I had to console myself with the thought that although I wasn't in control, perhaps someone, or something, else was.
Only one thing was certain in my brave new world.
The past.

The future was a blank book, which I now realised could be rewritten.

I was beginning to discover what Shakespeare had already known.

# Chapter Seven: Life

I had dozed off again.

It was now broad daylight.

And in that limbo between being asleep and awake I vaguely wondered where such an expression came from.

Then I was distracted: there was movement in the office.

It was probably that which woke me up.

The small hand on the office clock was now barely visible, but I could see it had just passed the very bottom of the dial.

It must be around 6 am.

I had yet to learn the prison routine, but I doubted I would be disturbed for a while.

They would see to their paperwork, probably over coffee and doughnuts, before dealing with their prisoner's breakfast.

Besides they had no doubt already checked on my condition while I was still asleep.

They may not particularly care about my welfare, but the death of an "alien" - especially a senior citizen - would not look well on their records.

It would certainly require a lot more unwelcome and unnecessary paperwork.

The air conditioning clicked back on, clearing some of the stale humidity left over from the night.

So I wrapped the blanket around me, curled up against the wall and went back into the safety of the past.

1985 to be precise.

The second time I was faced with a similar life or death dilemma was five years after the first.

In this instance it would be a completely different outcome.

Even after the experience with Joan I never considered myself or used the word "psychic."

Psychics for me are people who are open receptacles, and I never was.

Or I tried very hard not to be.

Despite the acknowledgement of, for want of a better word, my gift, I was not ready to accept everything which was thrown at me.

It was too painful and cost too much.

I had saved, but lost, one friend.

I cannot say I regretted the opportunity, or my decision, but I didn't want to encourage any more.

So for a long time I quite effectively blocked most of the messages sent to me.

A relatively easy task during my waking hours, but at night, when my defences were down.

You cannot control your dreams and that is exactly what happened.

At first I understood my weakness , my Achilles heel.

Night time and sleep were approached with, if not dread, at least some trepidation.

But time went by, and although I must have dreamt, they were the usual safe meaningless kind.

So eventually I fell back into the old ways, and five years later into the trap.

The first dream was so ordinary I didn't recognise it for what it was.

Now, with hindsight, it was different - so clear, so like my other experience.

But it was also pointless, it didn't make any sense.

It contained no one or no places I knew.

This time it began as a movie, rather than snapshots.

This time it was uncut - a straightforward narrative.

I was walking down a hospital corridor.

Alone: no one else was around.

It appeared to be daytime, or very bright artificial lighting.

There were no windows here.

This was unlike so many dreams where you are running but get nowhere.

I was walking towards a door at the end of the corridor: passing side doors on the way.

Suddenly I saw a man: late fifties; tall, well built but not overweight; greying hair - all the signs of middle age.

He emerged from one of the side doors on my right and crossed my path , without acknowledging my presence.

We were so close I was obviously invisible to him.

He turned to his right and joined the same path as myself.

I followed in his footsteps.

He reached the door at the end of the corridor, turned the old fashioned knob and entered.

I know this is a dream because it has a surreal quality about it, and I could pull myself free with very little effort.

But I don't want to.

I don't need to because I don't feel at all threatened.

So I went after my companion into the room at the end of the corridor.

It was a room empty save for one other occupant: an elderly woman who sat in one corner - and looked out of an extremely large sash window.

It looked like a sort of communal sitting room.

There were tables and chairs, but the woman sat in one of the high backed armchairs with a newspaper at her side.

It was daylight outside, and the sun streamed through the window.

But I saw her clearly.

White haired, painfully thin and frail I would have placed her around the mid eighties.

Despite her sad appearance now I felt she must have been quite stunning in her youth.

Her face still retained a timelessly beautiful profile.

The man approached her and I followed.

Everything was peaceful, so calm.

Even when the man came up behind her, opened the window and pushed her out.

I do wake up then, but I bring with me the last thing I saw.

The horrible smirk on his face.

So am I once again being asked to save a life?

This time a stranger, so what is the connection?

Why me - are all the real honest to God psychics tied up at the moment?

I don't know the woman, I don't know the man, and I certainly don't recognise the place,
Talk about mission impossible.
Except I do have a couple of important clues.
Somewhere in my dream, like the airport sign, I had seen the words "The Gables."
Unfortunately, I later find, it is one of the most common care home names.
Not surprising since all sorts of buildings, from most decades, have that distinctive architectural feature.
But I don't really have time to worry either about the reason I got this "assignment", or size of the task ahead of me.
For my other clue is a date, which I saw on the newspaper beside the woman.
I have just three days to find this place and save the woman.
I haven't even yet considered how exactly I am going to accomplish the latter, so I start on the first challenge.
"Suffice unto the day are the evils thereof;" (Matt 6:34)
As I said a common name, so I begin by limiting my search to the local area.
In the hope there is at least some method to this madness.
Now don't let's forget this was in the days before the world wide web.
All my research is done via the local library and a paper trail.
By noon the first day I find there are four homes which fit this category.
Of course there are no computers with websites for any prospective inmate to view.
Neither can I find any brochures - or illustrated advertisements which show any interiors.
So it's the old fashioned way, with a lot of footwork and a few white lies.
They are all in the suburbs - spread out to all points of the compass.
By the end of the first day I have managed to gain access to two of the institutions.
Neither resemble anything from my dream.

On the second day I hit a wall in that the third home I visit is not only the most distant but also the largest.

It takes me quite a while even to gain access, which I do on the pretence of an enquiry on behalf of an elderly relative.

Then instead of being allowed to informally inspect the facilities, I am treated to a guided tour.

A tour, I may say, worthy of the admission to a stately home - a rambling stately home at that.

Long before I leave I know this is another dead end.

Sorry no pun intended.

It is also too late to reach my final destination.

Again no pun intended.

It is desperation rather than humour, black or otherwise, which is making me foolish.

For tomorrow is the day when a woman is murdered and I am running out of time.

I have a good nights sleep: I have had no dreams since.

The message has been received and understood.

I am out of the house early and making my way to the fourth and last home on my list.

Even so it is almost noon and the residents, I am told, are at lunch.

Can I come back later?

Its not a question, so I find a local café and eat a snack I really do not want.

But there is something wrong.

There is no sun, instead the cloudy sky forecasts rain.

By the time I arrive back at the home this promise is fulfilled and it is dark.

Except for the corridor with the end door!

I am alone, the supervisor has told me, at this time of day, most patients are in their rooms with visiting family.

She leaves me to explore while she is called away.

I am back in my dream and begin walking towards the door.

When I reach the point where the man joined me I pause, just for a second.

Nothing happens.

So I continue alone,  open the door myself and go inside.

Its just as before:  tables, chairs and the woman sitting in a corner staring out a large window.

I don't know what to do,  but I cannot just leave, so I go across to her and begin to talk.

She is a truly lovely and charming lady.

She reminds so much of my grandmother.

There is no physical resemblance, but something deeper and stronger.

In the course of this conversation I discover she is waiting for her son.

With maternal pride she shows me his photograph.

Thankfully I was prepared for what I saw - the man in my dream.

As we talk the door opens and there stands the future murderer in the flesh.

After introductions I realise I cannot stay,  but neither can I leave.

Then thankfully the door opens again and a few other residents come in and settle themselves down for an afternoon of bridge.

I know I can safely leave now because the moment past,  but I am not even sure it was the right moment.

There is something else wrong, aside from the weather.

Then it comes to me:  there is no newspaper.

I go home, spending all the journey and rest of the evening going over and over the events.

Finally I go to bed and,  for the first time since the dream,  it is repeated.

I get up in the morning with only one thought: I must go back.

So I take another day off work with some feasible excuse and take the bus.

It is a beautiful day,  so unlike yesterday.

The sun is shining with no hint of a cloud,  which makes me nervous.

And I remember on my journey something else I learnt yesterday.

He is such a loving son - he comes every day.

I now know what is wrong, it really is so simple.

I check my watch, I am a little later than yesterday.

So, when my bus stops, I run back to the nursing home.

Same time, same place, different excuse.

I had promised to return as a visitor.

I am back in the corridor, walking towards the door, which I open.

My new friend is sitting staring out the window.

Exactly like the dream because a newspaper is now beside her, which shows yesterday's news.

It is otherwise deserted, and I entered so softly I have not disturbed her.

A few minutes later another visitor enters the room.

I watch him, but from a different angle.

He walks quietly across the room towards his unsuspecting mother.

For me the dream then returns, as all movement appears to morph into a slow motion replay - with one difference.

I watch as he throws open the window, and his mother cries out as he tries to grab her - before I step out from the door which has been hiding me.

I shout a warning, which his mother does not seem to hear, but he does.

It startles him and he spins around, losing his balance and falling back - through the window.

Its not something I had planned: taking a life as well as saving one.

Perhaps, although it was not my plan, it was always intended to happen.

If you are a believer - "the hand of God," if you are not Nemesis.

All I do know is it felt bloody good.

A later inquest, at which his mother, whom I now knew as Katherine Thompson, was the chief witness, revealed some interesting facts.

There had been a series of tragedies in the family.

These "accidents" had taken place in different locations - with different coroners.

The only common fact being they were all extremely advantageous to one particular party.

No prizes for guessing who!

His mother would have been the last in a long line of obstacles to his inheritance - which, with all the family deceased, was now quite substantial.

A sort of real life "Kind Hearts and Coroners," except his aim was not some sort of misplaced justice.

It was purely money!

After the inquest, which naturally I had to attend, I left the court satisfied, and vindicated, but guilty.

Not for my actions - I knew I would never lose any sleep over this mercenary sociopath's death.

But I did feel responsible for his mother.

After all, intended or not, I had taken away her only visitor.

Her son had removed the rest of her family!

So a week later I made the familiar journey to The Gables.

The sun was still shining but Mrs Thompson (Katherine) wasn't there - where I had always seen her.

It was little later than my two earlier visits - four if you count the dreams!

At first I was concerned then I heard a familiar voice calling my name.

She was sitting, at one of the tables, playing bridge with a group of her friends.

But she was facing the door and had seen me immediately, almost as though she was expecting a visitor.

She made her apologies, left them, and guided me to her private quarters.

Perhaps it was my imagination, or wishful thinking, but she seemed so much more alive, so much younger.

We sat down in a room which was a reflection of herself - clean, cosy, charming and full of her life.

I did notice, however, while there were many photographs none were of her son.

She probably noticed my actions, she may be old, but was sharp witted and observant.

If it is true that the eyes are the windows to the soul then hers was a very beautiful one indeed.

She offered me a chair and some refreshment.

She filled two glasses with brandy from her sideboard stash of beverages and sat down opposite me.

In many ways I was taken back to my last two meetings with Joan.

We sat in armchairs enjoying a comfortable silence for a few minutes before she broke it.

"I never liked him you know."

At first I wasn't quite sure what I had heard.

But she continued "Yes, he was my son, but there was always something not quite right" and she touched her temple.

"I hope you are too shocked."

I smiled and shook my head - as I said, I knew she was an intelligent woman.

No I was relieved.

I had not deprived her of anything.

Instead I had delivered her from a terrible dilemma.

One most mothers would feel knowing they had given birth to a monster.

Had she known of his earlier crimes?

I never asked her, but I think I knew the answer.

Perhaps that day at the window she had literally placed herself in God's hands.

And Katherine got me instead!

So I knew there were no regrets on either side about my intervention.

There was no guilt, no debt to pay.

So, it was for the best of all possible reasons, I began making my weekly visits.

Eventually these included trips to visit my grandmother and other excursions.

They continued until Katherine's death just three years later.

She wasn't alone when she died.

I held her hand as she whispered.

"God never closes a door but he opens a window".

# Chapter Eight:  Death

Five years later I found myself at another bedside, saying goodbye once more.

This time it was my precious grandmother.

Since the death of my grandfather it had just been the two of us.

I never married.

There had been plenty of opportunity but never enough temptation.

Or least never any emotion stronger than the bond between my "Gran" and I.

No other relationship could compete.

Some people would consider this sad,  but I felt just the opposite.

So many go through life without knowing real love at all  I could only feel blessed.

It had been a long goodbye.

My grandmother had begun developing the early symptoms of Alzheimer's ten years before her death.

At first it was just frequent forgetfulness and occasional confusion, especially in strange places.

In fact the first time I remember feeling any concern was on holiday.

We were staying in a static caravan near The New Forest.

It was the middle of the night and  I was awoken by my grandmother stumbling around in the dark.

She had been trying to find the toilet but she didn't appear to know where she was.

Not such a rare incident - many of us are disorientated while still under the influence of sleep.

Particularly true in unfamiliar surroundings.

In fact many people have died in such circumstances when the presence of stairs has not been recognised.

One well known case being that of Laura Ashley, who died following a fall while in her daughter's home.

Thankfully there are no stairs in a caravan.

So I consoled and deluded myself with all these quite rational excuses.

But I could not do so for long.

Another unusual circumstance, a few months later, confirmed something was wrong.

She tripped and fell in our kitchen.

Again not a cause for surprise or concern.

Falls are a fact of life as the spirit is still willing but the flesh becomes weaker.

And fortunately the strong bones in our genes usually protect us from more serious consequences.

But she had badly bruised her arm which, much against her wishes, was too swollen and painful to avoid further investigation..

Neither she, nor I, like hospitals.

In fact I imagine very few people do, but sometimes they are unavoidable.

Later that day the Emergency department referred to her a ward for overnight observation.

It was only one night, but it changed both our lives.

She never really recovered from this second, more traumatic, episode.

From that point her condition deteriorated quite rapidly.

Five years later - by the time she was introduced to Katherine, most of her short term memory was gone,

To the extent she quickly forgot Katherine's name or even remembered meeting her.

Certain other socially acceptable behaviour also disappeared, to the point many acquaintances found a variety of reasons not to revisit.

This behaviour was worst because it was not bizarre, it was just rude.

There was no longer any filtering connection between her brain and mouth.

I remember one occasion I invited a work colleague for lunch.

A slightly buxom lady who my grandmother greeted with "my goodness you're fat."

Real friends accept you for better or worse, and you quickly find out who these are in such circumstances.

Katherine may have been a late addition, but she was definitely a friend.

In those days mental illnesses were still taboo subjects: a cause for embarrassment.

Dementia was no different.

There were then no drugs which could cure or relieve the sufferer.

There were few support groups for the carers - who were usually relatives.

When there is nothing else left, talking helps to exorcise the demons.

Fear and ignorance.

But talking often seems an acceptance of the situation, and a strange sort of betrayal.

There were few to whom I could admit either.

Katherine was one of them.

Therapists, of course, have always known the benefits of unburdening, and many make a good living from it.

Like any other profession, some are good, some are bad, but neither were an option for me.

In the end I was too exhausted to do anything but exist.

When Katherine died that's virtually all I did for five more long, lonely, years.

Oh I had other friends, real friends, but that stiff upper lip stopped me asking for help.

During all these years my sensibilities seemed to go into hibernation.

I don't recall any more dreams or other premonitions, even those special feelings seemed to have departed.

But I believe such things are a part of nature, which knows what we can or cannot endure.

And I already had my hands full: caring for my grandmother and holding down a job.

Fortunately at that time I was self employed and working from home.

A mixed blessing.

On one hand a useful practical solution to my problem, but on the other, one which kept me even more isolated.

At the beginning of 1993 my grandmother had, to all intents and purposes, passed away.

My mother continued her yearly pilgrimage, which this year was been Easter and she had just returned home.

During her visit we had all suffered some sort of flu like virus, but even my grandmother now seemed to be on the mend.

Three days after my mother left my grandmother suffered a relapse and a doctor was called.

The prognosis was grim, though not unexpected.

It could be a day or a week, but this was now an end of life scenario.

As it happened it stretched out into the most "optimistic" estimate.

For a week, with the help of our GP , his nursing team and night time hospital nurses I kept her at home.

With hindsight it turned out to be a precious gift, which I would not have missed.

Emotional yes, but never sad.

It was a celebration of a life, which regretfully, all too often comes after death.

There were moments when, for the first time in many years, she was actually lucid.

In those intervals we talked a lot, catching up on all the time we had missed and making the most of the little time we had left.

My one comfort had always been in all those difficult years she had never once failed to recognise me.

Later, towards the end of that week, she became increasingly confused and agitated.

It seemed she was torn between what she would leave on earth and what awaited her in heaven.

Some cynics would put it down to the misfiring of a dying brain, but I thought I knew better.

That part of me, which for want to a better description I came to call my "extra sense" was waking up.

And, I would come to learn, it was returning refreshed and stronger than ever.

It was in those last two days, as she slipped in and out of consciousness, I felt she was also slipping in and out of her useless body.

Oh I don't mean she died or was having some sort of near death experience.

I could see her breathe, so her heart continued to beat.

But this was just a lingering force of habit.

She wasn't there.

Don't imagine I saw her spirit.

Besides she had always promised me I never would.

She knew my fear of such things.

Heredity may have given me some sort of psychic "gift," but not through choice!

I came to learn while I may not always be able to ignore this extra sense, I could control it a little.

And when it came to ghosts - well I really did not want to enter that realm.

There were, however, moments in the future when such beings were not so considerate as my dear grandmother!

So, up until that point I had my feelings and dreams.

All of which could be explained as anything other than the paranormal.

This was something different.

No I didn't see anything and no other sensations which came through the normal channels.

As a rational explanation I could use the following analogy.

Everyone knows that the loss of one sense, will turn the other four into over drive.

But in my case, it seems, when my extra sense needs power it turns off the other five.

Why had I not noticed this before?

Simple - my previous experience had been through dreams.

You do not use your ears, eyes, nose, tongue or fingers in dreams.

Instead you use that unconsciousness which scientists attribute to the brain, but many believe to be the soul.

As for me, well I do not have enough knowledge or faith to argue either theory.

But I had learnt to trust my feelings, as I had always trusted my grandmother.

So in those quiet moments, while we were alone, I felt her presence.

Which had no connection with the almost spent body on the bed next to me.

So mock or ridicule, but remember as you do, such actions are almost always the mind's response to fear.

Just as a nervous laugh is the physical reaction to stress and anxiety.

So make up your own minds.

At some point we all have to.

I have grown too old and, hopefully a little wiser, to waste much time or effort in pointless argument.

I have accepted my own truths.

So back to a bright Sunday morning in the spring of 1993, when my grandmother and I said our last goodbye.

At least on this earth.

It was perfect, as though it was always meant to be.

Just the two of us quietly holding hands.

At peace: nothing left unsaid and no deeds left undone.

I told her I loved her, which she was to carry to my grandfather, although I knew he wasn't very far away.

She took a small final breath and slipped completely away.

The overwhelming feeling was relief.

For both of us.

This isn't to say it was easy or painless.

Grief is beyond reason and loss inconsolable.

Then I remembered words from an incredible book which described my feelings at that precise moment.

In Wuthering Heights Emily Bronte describes such overwhelming heartbreak through Heathcliffe when he says of

Catherine's death:

"I cannot live without my life.
 I cannot live without my soul."

# Chapter Nine:  Light


But of course I did live.

And here I am now sitting in this cell to prove it.

The building has woken up.

I have been provided with breakfast - I suspect courtesy of a local take out.

At 8am I was given a menu - and about fifteen minutes later was handed a paper bag containing the requested "biscuits."

Thank goodness over the years my transAtlantic trips have taught me the deviations in our shared language!

So for biscuits read a sort of unsweetened scone,  which in the absence of an English teatime, are eaten with every other meal.

I suppose an alternative to toast for breakfast and bread roll for dinner.

While I cannot say I enjoy most of the popular fast food in America, I do really love the biscuits.

Those in my bag were lavishly spread with some fat, which was pleasant enough,  but I could easily believe was not butter!

But when you have few luxuries left in life such comforts are better than fine dining.

Certainly better than the meagre dishes usually served up in many gastro pubs.

Apart from some basic essential communication no one says much to me.

To be fair maybe they are having the same language problems with me I have with them.

On any of my trips below the Mason Dixon line,  it always takes me a while to acclimatise to the slower speech.

Otherwise known as the " Southern drawl".

But on previous visits,  after a few days,  I have adapted so successfully that by the time I return to New York I know exactly how southerners feel!

The speech patterns are so fast it makes our common language incomprehensible.

For  the moment I am still in my native English tongue,  which tends to either charm or confuse.

I love the South but the pace of living and language does take some adjustment.

So until this happens I opt for the bizarre approach usually applied when trying to converse with foreigners.

If you speak English slowly and loudly enough suddenly you will become intelligible.

At least in this instance there was a fighting chance of making some progress!

And I do although this method probably does not endear me to the officers.

Who either think I am one of those eccentric Brits,  or just bloody rude.

Probably both!

For the moment though I am alone:   to eat and enjoy my meal in peace.

I doesn't take long and once again I am left to my own devices, my own thoughts.

Hospitals and prisons are both institutions, and while one is in existence to serve the individual, the other is in place to serve society.

However they do have many similarities.

They share the tendency to treat inmates as mushrooms.

Or,  with apologies, as my blunt paternal ancestors in Yorkshire would say;  "keep them in the dark and feed them shit."

Probably not their fault.

They are dealing with the old problem:   too many customers and not enough staff.

However frustrating this may be for the latter,  it is ten times worst for the vulnerable individuals at their mercy!

With regard to hospitals I have always maintained every surgeon, doctor and nurse should be made to endure a week as a anonymous patient to really appreciate this.

Hospital administrators should serve a months incarceration.

For politicians my sentence would be six months!

All in the general wards of course - not private suites.

It may be time consuming in the short term, but the benefits in morale, job satisfaction and shorter recovery times would more than compensate.

Stepping down off my soapbox, once more I make the point this digression is not irrelevant.

There is a saying that "the mills of God grind slowly."

That being the case then the gears of hospitals and prisons sometimes seem to have gone into reverse.

For the past two days I had been promised, and still awaited, news from outside.

I didn't have a lawyer, but couldn't complain because I had not requested one.

But I was expecting news from another quarter.

Which would either release me or, in this state, leave me in prison for years with the eventual prospect of death by lethal injection.

In my count the authorities had another 24 hours to detain me.

I had been advised that detention without charge is 72 hours in this country.

If charged then all bets are off.

Because I have also been advised imprisonment while awaiting trial can vary between 90 and 175 days - sometimes beyond!

So much for the concept of "innocent until proven guilty."

None of this is a safe topic for contemplation.

So I retreat once more to the safety of the past.

# Chapter Ten:  Darkness

July 1993

A few months since my grandmother's death.

By this time most people had assumed I should have "got over" my bereavement, and had returned to their own lives.

But a few, who had experienced loss themselves, continued to give their support and love.

They knew grief does not disappear and it takes a long time for the pain to dull, if indeed it ever does.

I had my work to occupy my thoughts during the day.

The nights were another matter.

Fortunately it was summer so evenings were long and the actual hours of darkness short.

By the time I went to bed, in a house full of memories, but little else, I made certain I was exhausted.

It was not a difficult plan.

There was plenty to keep me occupied.

After many years of secretarial office work, I was now a freelance picture researcher.

Just in case, like me before I became one, you wonder what a picture researcher is.

Then the clue is in the job title.

Basically it involves researching, and obtaining permissions for book illustrations.

I began as a clerical assistant to a picture researcher, whose work load became so overwhelming I soon found myself with my own projects.

From that moment on I had found a career I loved.

The fact it was a well paid one was a bonus.

Eventually I swapped self employment in a publishing house, for self employment at home.

The transition, thanks for once to technology, was effortless and came at the right moment to juggle the demands of home and work.

While I cannot claim to have enjoyed a perfect or celebrated life, I have been lucky.

A gift never to be underestimated, which Napoleon knew when he famously asked; "I know he's a good general, but he is lucky?"

So once again it was one of those moments in my life when fate was on my side.

And, even if I say so myself, I did the job well, which led to more and more commissions.

So the long days were filled with work, highly profitable work.

Any extra daylight hours were devoted to a love shared by my grandmother and myself.

We both loved "pottering" around in the garden.

Although its size was such, it was more like a full time occupation than a spare time hobby.

So the long summer passed, the nights began drawing in, and the garden no longer required so much attention.

Of course my paid work was not dependant on the season or time of day.

It just meant more hours to fill, particularly when the autumn weather prevented any outdoor activity.

But by that time I had found myself another "interest."

Or rather it found me, and I was not very enthusiastic about it in the beginning.

It began sadly with news of another death, and an unexpected one.

At least as far as I was concerned.

Joan had apparently been diagnosed with lung cancer two years previously.

The aggressive nature of this type of the disease, meant it was not a good prognosis.

Nevertheless Joan chose to undergo an equally aggressive treatment - hoping, but I suspect knowing, it would never be a cure.

It was a choice taken for the same reason she listened to me thirteen years earlier.

Joan had a great lust for life and would not go down without a fight.

I knew nothing about any of this.

As I guessed we would never resume our close friendship.

Any communication had been restricted to birthday and Christmas cards.

She had not even told me she was ill.

Something which hurt.

But I understood - I may probably have done the same in the circumstances.

Even if our history had been different, it is still the case that terminal illness carries with it many concerns beyond the physical.

The fear an illness which is threatening your future will also steal away your present.

The knowledge that once the diagnosis is known no one will see you in the same way.

You will no longer be family, friend or colleague you will be defined by the disease.

You will be judged by your looks: too pale; too drawn; too tired; too thin.

Conditions we all suffer, from time to time!

Even your behaviour: so short tempered, so depressed, so brave will be put down to the illness rather than normal human emotions.

When all you really want to do is be treated like "you", and forget for a while the difference.

So it hurt, may not necessarily be true, but was understood.

It was left to a mutual friend, Margaret, to tell me all the details of her death and arrangements.

There was some consolation in the fact Joan had specifically asked I be told and invited to the funeral.

This was to take place in her new home near Bath.

I would not need to book any accommodation, thanks to the M4 it was only a 90 minute drive.

It was a day trip I had made, usually with American tourists in tow, many times.

Joan had chosen a cremation rather than a burial and I was surprised the service took place in a church.

I never remember Joan being a church goer, in fact she used to joke she was a "four wheel Christian."
Meaning whose only attendance was in a pram(Christening); limo (wedding) and hearse (funeral.)
I think she was a little hard on herself.
She had never, to my knowledge. been a practising churchgoer, but was one of the best and kindest people I knew.
I couldn't help but wonder if her later "conversion" had anything to do with our shared experience.
Perhaps a way to come to terms with the whole experience and perhaps alleviate some survivor's guilt.
Margaret was waiting at the church when I drove up.
After greeting, and asking about each other's health and lives, our conversation naturally turned to our friend.
We agreed she had been a wonderfully special person, and shared the usual confusion and anger she had been taken far too soon.
But I did not share the consolation it could have been a much shorter span.
I doubted Joan herself had shared this knowledge with anyone else.
As it turned out I was completely wrong.
We went inside with a large group of mourners as the hearse pulled into the church gates.
There were a few family members, but no husband or children.
So the front row of pews in the small church was only partial occupied.
A few brave souls, probably those hard of hearing and sight, took up positions immediately behind the nearest and dearest.
The rest of us typically behaved like children in a classroom, or courting couples in a cinema, and jostled for positions in the back row.
Late comers filled in the gap.
It was a short but emotional service.
The usual programme of prayers, two well chosen, well known hymns and a personal eulogy by a family member.
There was nothing resembling a sermon, just a short address by

the resident vicar.

A short rotund cheery man, who had a deep naturally warm voice, instead of the dreary drone often adopted in such circumstances.

Joan and I used to joke such clergy must have missed the class in empathy at theological college.

Rather like doctors who have no bedside manner.

I smiled at the recollection and looked at the coffin as it was carried out.

She wasn't there.

We followed the hearse to the crematorium, where our friendly minister concluded his service.

As we silently filed past the coffin, a few, either much closer or more emotional, touched or kissed the lid.

Neither Margaret nor I joined them

We had both said our goodbyes earlier, in my case a long time ago.

Besides neither of us were brought up to be demonstrative creatures.

Old school - our feelings were private.

We did not wear our hearts on our sleeves.

But they were no less sincere, perhaps all the more so.

In this age where every emotion is a matter of public display, such calm acceptance is not considered healthy.

But everyone grieves in their own way, and I am not convinced a violent unburdening of emotion is always a very beneficial, or often even genuine response.

As I said everyone grieves in their own way, and should be allowed to do so.

A funeral, after all, is not for the benefit of the departed, it is for the comfort of the bereaved.

However I have to admit shedding a silent tear or two, as the music played Joan's final selection from South Pacific: "Younger than springtime."

I glanced across at Margaret as we left the crematorium, and saw she shared its significance.

It was the last film we had all seen together.

As a matter of form we followed the mourners to view the floral tributes, although neither of us had contributed.

We both preferred to honour the dead by helping the living.

Everyone has to earn a living, but sadly for them, this did not include florists.

Instead we donated funds to Joan's two favourite charities: which were divided equally between two and four legged beneficiaries.

As we walked back to our respective cars Margaret told me there was a wake at a nearby pub.

Honestly I would have preferred to make my apologies and begin the journey home, but something about the invitation made refusal difficult.

Something more than just the opportunity for old friends to catch up.

Thankfully it was a good old fashioned pub, so the buffet was substantial - not just finger food.

Nothing wrong with sandwiches and sausage rolls.

But it was a bitterly cold day and the addition of soup and jacket potatoes was a thoughtful gesture.

Afterwards we shared a pot of tea, although I did think I may later regret the second cup.

I really didn't want to have to stop on the way back.

As we sipped our drinks in what should have been a comfortable silence I began to realise it was anything but.

By the time I made my excuses and stood up to leave it became more and more obvious.

Margaret either didn't appear to hear, or refused to take the hint.

Instead she sat staring down at the floor, apparently transfixed by something I could not see.

Then I realised she wasn't actually looking at anything.

She was thinking: trying to find the right words to begin.

After a few more awkward moments, which felt much longer, she finally looked up at me.

She had obviously decided on the direct approach.

"Joan told me what happened in 1980."

So I was wrong about our little secret: at least as far as Margaret was concerned.

Perhaps it had been revealed, innocently, under the influence of alcohol during a girl's night out.

Or maybe it was later, unconsciously, as a result of morphine administered by the hospice.

It didn't really matter Joan and I had never made any pact of secrecy.

But it just seemed strange Margaret would wait until now to start this conversation.

I sat down again, because I realised this was the beginning, not the end, of her request.

Because that's exactly what it was.

She wanted help, the problem was I am not sure I could provide it.

Margaret had been a single parent of an only child, a daughter, for many years.

Her husband had died in a road accident when she was just a baby.

Like my grandmother and I they had always been extremely close.

But now Debbie was a teenager and going through all the usual physical and emotional upheavals.

Most youngsters get through the experience unscathed, but in this case there was another worrying factor.

His name was Craig.

He was every daughter's dream and every mother's nightmare! At least that was how Margaret felt about him.

Although she admitted she may be just a little biased.

He was an American, that was not the problem.

The problem was he seemed to be a pathological liar.

Someone who lies for no reason, no apparent motive.

Margaret had caught him out on several occasions.

He either laughed it off, or lied about what he had said.

Unfortunately, but predictably, Debbie could, or would, not see any faults in him.

He was, Margaret warned, admittedly charming.

No change there.

How many G.I. brides had been sold similar stories of the American dream courtesy of a smart uniform, nylon stockings and a diet of glamorous Hollywood films?

Only to discover, too late, that their future home was a shack in the swamps instead of the promised Southern mansion.

So what was my old friend's request?

I tell her straight away I cannot promise anything.

But she says no she understands (which is more than I have ever done), but please could I just meet him.

See what I think - or more accurately "feel."

Obviously Joan's description of my abilities went beyond the dream episode.

So I do at least make that promise.

I could not refuse, besides my curiosity is now roused, enough to want to meet this "problem."

Although I do have one concern.

I have never before tried to control those instinctive feelings about people.

They have just come.

I am hoping pressure does not affect the accuracy of my "character reading."

Margaret, it turns out, has already made plans on expectation of my agreement.

Craig is a regular visitor at the house, and next Sunday has accepted an invitation for lunch.

To which I am also invited.

My old friend has been wise enough to understand the pitfalls of opposition.

While she never encouraged the relationship she had been careful to avoid outright disapproval.

A dangerous tightrope to walk, and one which makes me grateful I never had children.

They may be a blessing, but it is a two edged sword: they can also break your heart.

A week later, when I meet Craig, I wonder how she can bear the pretence and why he doesn't see through it.

Perhaps it is simply such self absorbed people don't see, let alone care about, the feelings of others.

My fears of failure were unjustified.

From the moment I met him I loathed him.

A strong word, but none other would do.

He was truly poisonous, so much so I would rather have held a viper than his hand.

But I took it, a cold and lifeless thing, which suddenly tightened and gripped my hand.

The action shocked and unnerved me.

In my experience you do not grasp a stranger's hand so violently unless you are trying to make a point.

We locked stares and once again the serpent analogy came to me.

He had the most awful soulless eyes.

Rescue came in the form of Margaret summoning us all to the table.

She had warned me to come hungry.

Good advice since it was a traditional Sunday spread: roast beef with all the trimmings.

A meal I usually love, but in this case, one I could not do justice.

There was even something about the way he ate which turned my stomach.

He devoured every morsel, like some starving predator.

All the while looking at Debbie, who sat across the table, next to me.

I don't know how Margaret felt, but I was fighting the strongest urge to smother him with the Yorkshire pudding!

But the worse was to come, while I was still trying to digest a hearty slice of apple pie and custard.

Margaret had just poured out cups of coffee, or in my case tea, when Craig gave an announcement.

Perhaps he was after all not so insensitive: he waited until his hostess had put down the kettle.

Apparently the couple, for such they now presented themselves, had another "surprise."

They were planning a future together, which would begin three thousand miles away, in his homeland.

He then droned on and on about a large piece of real estate which had been left to him by his now deceased parents.

He described it as a residence worthy of J R Ewing, and once again I thought of all those young gullible post war brides.

As I watched Debbie, I could not bear to look at her mother or Craig for very different reasons, I was stunned.

How could she believe all this twaddle?

She was not stupid, but two old sayings suddenly came to mind: "you cannot put an old head on young shoulders," and "love is blind."

Like most proverbs these have a basis in fact, but are ones with time and experience she could outgrow.

I doubted at this precise moment she even knew what real love was.

Something I think her fiance was counting on!

Then I had the most monstrous thought.

Perhaps after all he was not a pathological liar - because he had a motive for all his lies.

And she was now sitting next to him, trustingly holding that same hand I had found so repulsive.

Debbie.

# Chapter Eleven: Despair

There were a few half hearted congratulations before the "happy couple" left to visit friends - hers not his.

As far as I was aware he had none.

At least none he had mentioned.

Why am I not surprised?

Who could stand his manufactured charm for long?

Who would fail to see beneath the superficial shell?

Well Debbie apparently.

I actually began to consider the possibility of some mind changing drug.

But, no, it was a lot simpler than that.

She thought she was in love and he had done everything to encourage that.

She had come from a loving home, the more so because it was concentrated within mother and daughter.

But sometimes that can be a disadvantage because if you grow up without understanding evil you do not recognise it.

Not everyone has my sensitive nose for trouble!

Debbie had been nurtured in a protective atmosphere where she thrived.

In many ways it was a perfect upbringing, but not a safe introduction to the real world.

Of course, Margaret being a sensible woman, had warned the child about the danger of taking sweets from a stranger or getting into a car with them.

But she had not made it clear demons come in many disguises, if they are clever.

Most are.

And I think this particular beast was a genius of his kind.

Of course I had been brought up in similar circumstances.

But my grandmother was older than Margaret and understood the wisdom of a broad education.

One which included exposure to unpleasant truths.

Not all devils come with horns and a tail, smelling of sulphur.

The most successful arrive in Armani suits with the scent of

Christian Dior!

Besides while I was brought up in a loving home, I was always aware that my life could have taken a completely different route.

A very bumpy and potholed road.

A path strewn with guilt and recrimination for something I could not help.

The crime of having been born.

All this passes my mind as I sit in the living room while Margaret shows her guests to the door.

The person who comes back is completely different to the person who welcomed me just a few hours ago.

How could someone have aged so quickly?

My friend looks suddenly old, frail, and, worse, utterly defeated.

And for myself - I am literally speechless.

I really don't know what to say or do.

I cannot possibly relate to her grief.

I have never given birth to a child, whose loss I am suddenly expected, not only to accept, but actually celebrate.

And such a loss to such a person!

So I do not have the right to offer meaningless platitudes.

But I can understand her frustration and anger, because I see both emotions in her face.

These I can share.

She comes over and sits down on the sofa next to me.

I don't even feel I can make any physical contact.

As I said earlier we have never been touchy feely.

I suppose this is the drawback to that British "stiff upper lip" reserve.

But she leans against my shoulder and the barrier is broken.

I hug her while she sobs.

I promise we will think of something, which seems to give her some hope.

A good thing she cannot read my thoughts because I have absolutely no ideas.

After a while, and another pot of tea, we console ourselves with the fact that we do have one ally.

Time is on our side.

Or so we thought.

When I leave an hour later, I do so with the assurance I will 'phone tomorrow.

After a good night's rest.

That night is dreamless, and the worst sleep I have had for months!

The only plan I can come up with is the old "best line of defence is attack" strategy.

We agree it would be a mistake to approach Debbie.

Tempting as it is, we know such a scheme would play into Craig's hands.

It would only antagonise her and add determination to her infatuation.

But there is another choice.

Hopefully the two of us are wrong about his character.

Hard as it may be - we should try to give him the benefit of the doubt.

So Margaret gives me the contact details for two of her daughter's closest friends, and I work out a good cover story for my approach.

Its not hard.

The truth often really is the best policy.

So I decided to simply ask them what they thought about the relationship.

Worse scenario: they could tell Debbie.

Even worse scenario: they could tell Craig.

But in either event this would only blackened my name and leave Margaret blameless.

And if they wondered where I obtained their names?

Well Debbie had mentioned them during the lunch.

They would probably never ask her, and she would probably never remember.

Craig, of course, would.

It may put him on his guard, but I doubted he would say anything.

Besides I was willing to take the risk.

As everything turned out all this was a waste of time and brain power.

It took just two telephone conversations to discover the best and worst of the situation.

Our feelings about Craig were confirmed: her friends mistrusted and disliked him as much as we did.

Their first instincts had matched mine, but they had been less diplomatic and because of this neither had seen Debbie in weeks.

In fact none of her friends had seen her alone since Craig appeared on the scene.

Standard behaviour for such predators.

Identify the weakest, or most vulnerable, of the group and then isolate them.

But it did raise the worrying question "where were they going when they left Sunday?"

And it left me with the task of telling Margaret, not only our fears were justified, but her daughter had become an accomplished liar.

Before I could do so, she rang me.

She sounded absolutely distraught.

So much so I jumped in the car and made the ninety minute trip to Bath in under seventy.

Not the safest journey with my mind going over and over what Margaret had finally managed to tell me.

Something had happened.

Something neither of us had foreseen in our darkest thoughts.

Ironically though something which answered my earlier question.

The moment they left us on Sunday they had gone to the airport and caught a plane to New York.

Margaret had not suspected a thing until this moment when she received a phone call from her ecstatic, and recently married, daughter.

And the reason why her mother had suspected nothing?

Because Debbie, had made a telephone call from the airport saying she was staying over at a friend's house for a couple of nights!

A cruel trick, and completely unworthy of Debbie and all the years of love and sacrifice devoted to her.

But lust, which so many people mistake for love, may not be blind, but it is blinkered.

It only sees what the ego wants it to.

I could not excuse Debbie, but I could see Craig's signature all over it.

When I arrived at the house the front door was unlocked, and I remembered how people will leave open a cage for a lost bird to return.

I found Margaret sitting on Debbie's bed clutching a once loved and now abandoned teddy bear.

She later told me she could not accept it until she had entered her daughter's bedroom, to find her passport gone and wardrobe empty.

Only a few things remained - remnants of her childhood, like the bear.

I remained overnight, out of concern for my friend rather than her selfish daughter, who I felt had now made her bed and deserved to lie in it.

Of course I never made this particular sentiment known to Margaret.

As I said, I am not a mother, but I do know their strengths and weaknesses.

No mother would accept the guilt of her child - except probably mine!

Neither of us had a very restful night.

Margaret because she could not sleep and myself, because she could not sleep.

Several times I heard her wandering around like a lost soul, always settling in her daughter's bedroom.

She was obviously trying to come to terms with her loss.

Grief is not an emotion confined to the death of a loved one, and sometimes death is the more acceptable option.

I left later the next day when a closer family friend arrived.

Someone more qualified than I to offer the emotional support she now needed.

I had to leave.

I would be an unpleasant constant reminder, just as I had been to Joan.

Neither was my fault.

But I could no more banish guilt than Margaret could banish grief.

In this instance the die was already cast even before I entered this home.

We hugged on the doorstep and she whispered a meaningless "thank you."

I knew then, looking back at the house, it had changed since Sunday.

It was no longer a home, and I knew Margaret would not be able to stay here.

It could not be a shrine to her daughter.

It was a thing of the past and my friend had to think of the future.

Debbie was still alive and where there is life there is hope.

# **Chapter Twelve: Hope**

We kept in touch until six months later when she left to find her child.

By then, as I anticipated, the house and contents were sold, and she had cut all ties to this country.

I never heard from her again, although not a day passed without thinking about her.

Another six months after that, with summer once again over, and new projects few and far between, I was looking for another distraction.

I am a great believer in "cometh the hour cometh the man", although in this case it wasn't a man.

It was a young, slight and slender woman.

But there is another saying, somewhat at odds with my own role in publishing, "you should never judge a book by its cover."

With my grandmother's guidance I can honestly say I never took anything, or anyone, at face value.

So when I first met this young lady, during a team building exercise at a local hotel, I had no preconceptions based on gender or age.

This is not to say, however, there was no reaction.

My old tried and trusted vibes were oscillating like an electric toothbrush - for want of a more dubious parallel!

I had never met anyone, since my grandmother, who produced such a strong positive response.

Little did I know it at the time, but this encounter was to be the start of my third career.

Although it was one which would never make me rich or famous.

This was my own decision.

Somehow I had always believed I should never seek payment for my special legacy.

It was given to me: I felt I could not charge for sharing it with others.

But many times over the next years I have received gifts, which I could not refuse.

All of them more valuable to me than even the largest cheque.

But for now back to that autumn and a meeting which would change several lives.

Many of them are tales for another time and place, but the first is essential to this story.

Over lunch Elizabeth, for this was my new acquaintance's name, and I talked about our work.

It turned out we were both freelance picture researchers, but at either end of our respective careers.

We compared our experiences and shared our concerns about the course.

Both agreeing that it is difficult, if not impossible, to fit into a team if you are not included.

Then she asked if I ever had problems matching illustrations to books.

So often she explained she had found the perfect choice only to have it declined by the publishers.

To be truthful my answer was no.

Part of my gift was the ability to just know which painting or photograph would appeal to a particular author or editor.

I remember once saying to a certain editor "now I know you don't like Henry Moore, but I think you will like this."

Well I was right, even though there was no way I knew his general dislike for that artist, or why he would like this - which he did.

It was that simple, but how could I tell Elizabeth?

As it turned out I didn't need to.

Because her next words completely silenced me.

"You know sometimes I have this strange connection to people - like I know what they are feeling, perhaps I just need to trust that."

Thank goodness the sessions then resumed and we went to our separate groups.

The afternoon exercises with large Lego bricks were fun but, for me, absolutely pointless.

But it did give me the opportunity to think, and go back over the lunch time conversation.

The day wound up at 6pm, when everyone set off in their different directions.

I suspect leaving without any difference to their attitudes, or any intention to change.

But a good time seemed to have been had by all, certainly a good lunch.

In the car park I met up with Elizabeth, who was looking more than a little annoyed.

Her boyfriend had agreed to pick her up, but had just telephoned to say he would be delayed an hour.

It was growing dark, and cold, so I suggested we retire back to the bar for drink.

As I was driving home, it was my usual soft drink, but Elizabeth insisted on paying so she could indulge in a brandy.

Alcohol is a great liberator, so she talked while I listened.

Like myself our lunchtime chat had obviously preyed on her mind because she now resumed that topic.

She began by apologising for her remarks, and then apologised for going on about it.

Then she went on to explain why these curious feelings were so much on her mind.

She had recently met an author and for no apparent reason felt suddenly anxious and uncomfortable.

It was something she had never experienced before, and it worried her.

The odd thing being she wasn't afraid of him, but she just knew he was terrified of her.

Yet no one else at the meeting had seen it.

She apologised yet again, and shaking her head said "you must think I am mad."

I reassured her with a little white lie, and told her most of us occasionally get such irrational feelings.

I ended mixing a little fact with a lot of fiction by revealing the story of my teenage party, without the chilling punch line.

I didn't want to frighten her, but neither did I want her to disregard those messages.

They were always sent for a reason.

I was fascinated - it was the first time in my life I had met a kindred spirit.

Now it looked as if there were two.

Because what had the man seen in Elizabeth which had scared him so?

I would soon find out because she had given me his name.

It was done innocently enough: two colleagues exchanging shared experiences.

# Chapter Thirteen: Dream

Dr Kevin Lambert was a lecturer of medieval history at the local university, and my own instinct told me I needed to speak to him.

As soon as possible.

I still remembered the last time I had tried to mess with the future!

So the next morning I rang the number I had found for the humanities department.

In my experience early calls are probably the best time to catch an academic.

An hour or so to stock up on caffeine and croissants before the demands of colleagues or students intervene.

It's a hard life!

I have also found most are reasonable creatures, with some well known exceptions.

Those who seem to think, since they believe to have proven there is no God, they can move into the vacancy.

Despite these few over the years I have made some good friends among the community.

But I have learnt most have one quirk - they do not suffer fools gladly.

Perhaps because they are surrounded by so many of them?

Although I have one myself, courtesy of The Open University, a degree does not guarantee intelligence, certainly not common sense.

But I digress.

I rang and was surprised to be immediately transferred to the Dr Lambert's extension.

Sometimes departmental secretaries can compete with doctors receptionists as protective pit bulls.

My luck held.

The call was quickly answered by someone I could not equate with weakness, let alone fear.

Dr Lambert had a strong deep voice, which was neither abrupt nor hesitant.

It was a calm, pleasing introduction to a man whose tone seemed to indicate a down to earth sense of humour.

I hoped I was right.

For some reason I felt I could not afford to make a mistake this time.

I apologised for the early call, then went into my pitch.

Most of it true, with just a little fabrication.

Yes I was a picture researcher, yes I was a freelancer working for an academic publisher, yes I was trying to arrange a meeting.

But no it wasn't to discuss the illustrations for his new book.

It was all feasible and didn't link me to his meeting with Elizabeth.

She had already told me she had refused the commission.

She couldn't work with someone who looked at her as though she had just stepped out of his worst nightmare.

So it was reasonable, and not entirely untruthful, to suggest I had been given his name by a colleague.

He quickly agreed a time and place.

Later that day in his room at the university.

But before we broke the connection had I detected just a hint of relief?

Now I only had a very short time to worry about my plan and its outcome.

I turned up as arranged and was directed to his office.

I was already acquainted with the university, which was an ancient institution, and one I loved.

While I understand the inclination for new buildings to reflect their period, my preference, as with pubs, was for the traditional.

They had an atmosphere I doubted any of the modern concrete and glass minimalist buildings would every acquire.

Perhaps it was just another instance of my sensitivity, but the ancient stones and old wood seemed to contain centuries of life - and death.

A place every self respecting ghost could haunt.

There were some carbuncle late additions, but I was pleased to see that Dr Lambert's building was appropriate for a history scholar.

A wonderful gabled stone building erected before Henry VIII's first scaffold.

Once inside his room was accessed by a small stone spiral staircase, obviously designed to deter any unwelcome armed invaders.

For me it just got better and better.

I found his inner sanctum protected by a thick oak door and knocked on it.

Instead of the usual "come in" response the door opened and Dr Lambert stood in front of me.

Exactly as I had imagined him.

Although not quite: he was surprisingly young for an academic author.

In fact he was probably the first author who was actually younger than myself.

But it did explain his lack of ego, and sense of humour.

For I could see he had a very developed one.

His aura definitely fell on the side of the angels.

I liked him immediately, which made me all the more determined to help him if I could.

He invited me to sit down and share a pot of tea with a plate of fresh cream cakes.

Not something again I am normally used to when discussing book illustrations.

Although I did once have such an experience while researching at Novosti Press (a Soviet press agency).

Some of the most generous and welcoming people I have ever met, and completely contradicting the stereotype.

Another case of never taking anyone, at face. or propaganda value.

But I was not there to make a political point, or discuss the merits of éclairs versus Belgium buns.

However it's a good way to start, so I help myself to the latter and begin.

I commenced on safe ground discussing his latest book, and suggested list of internal illustrations (again courtesy of Elizabeth).

By the time I refused my second stack of calories and we moved on to the book jacket, I judged the moment was right.

For the first time I mention Elizabeth, in, what I considered, a very natural and matter of fact way.

It's a simple remark repeating her ideas for a possible cover design.

But her name has an astonishing effect on my teatime companion.

Kevin - as he asked me to call him - froze in mid mouthful and suddenly I had an inkling of what Elizabeth had seen.

All the youthful exuberance and joie de vivre had gone, or at least was well hidden.

It was probably still there, somewhere, beneath a shroud of exhaustion and fear.

Because that's all I saw now.

And an expression, which I could only describe with a remembered quote from Tennyson - and memorialised by Agatha Christie:

"Out flew the web and floated wide
The mirror crack'd from side to side
'the curse has come upon me' said,
The Lady of Shalott."

It may sound a little dramatic, but that's exactly how he looked "cursed."

Such an extraordinary reaction to such an ordinary comment.

Of course even if I had wanted to change the subject and defuse the situation I could not.

Its what I had come for.

So, although I felt more than a little guilty for being the cause of all this misery, I carried on.

"Is something wrong?"

Stupid question, which really required no answer, and for a

short while he gave none.
I was worried the moment would pass and this would have been for nothing.
Then he turned to look me in the eye and said:
"I don't know - but you do don't you."
Not a question - a challenge.
One I had to answer, and one I hoped he would believe because was the only one I had.
It was the truth.
So I began my explanation and confession.
When I finished, there was no reproach, but best of all, no doubt.
He just smiled weakly and said:
"Thank God: I thought I was going mad."

I smiled back and replied: "If so you're not the only one.
Elizabeth said exactly the same thing, but what was it about her that upset you so?"
Then he began his story.

# Chapter Fourteen : Nightmare

Like some of the worst and best things in life, it came seemingly out of nowhere about two weeks ago.
The day had been like every other.
Nothing to distinguish it from the day before, but that night it began.
No warning, no premonition.
He had always been a good sleeper.
A classic example of falling asleep before his head hit the pillow.
Like everyone he dreamt.
Like most of us he didn't remember many of them.
But this one he couldn't forget.
It started as a dream and ended as a nightmare, which had been repeated every night since.
It was so real and intense every morning he woke up sweating and in a panic.
No wonder he looked, excuse the expression, absolutely knackered!
As someone who had "been there and bought the T shirt" I had a little understanding and a lot of sympathy.
After my own sleep deprivation experience I knew exactly how he felt.
The only surprise was how he had managed to conceal this so successfully.
When I heard the details of his nightmare many other things began to fall into place.
It always started innocently enough.
He was in the backseat of a car.
For some reason he couldn't see the driver, but somehow knew there was one.
There was also a fellow passenger.
Someone sitting next to him, but all he could make out was a dark outline.
It seemed to be night.

So far there was no feeling of unease: no sense of threat.
Then suddenly his world is turned upside down - quite literally.
Kevin realised the vehicle was now resting on its roof.
That's when the nightmare really began.
There is some argument about whether or not the sense of smell is possible in dreams.
Something most scientists dispute.
They argue any perceived scents come from an external source: flowers in the bedroom or coffee on the stove.
However Kevin swore that the next thing he remembered was the smell of burning.
Specifically the choking stench of hot rubber and melting plastic, and something else - petrol.
He felt completely disorientated and realised he was lying on the roof of what was apparently a taxi.
He could see the meter, which was still illuminated, but the driver had gone.
He suddenly remembered the third person and fumbled around in the darkness, now made more challenging and terrifying by the smoke.
At first nothing and then his fingers connected with a foot.
A very small foot: a woman's.
Then so many things seemed to happen at once.
A woman screamed.
The sound of glass cracking.
A gush of black choking smoke.
Then there was light.
But it was not a healthy white radiance.
It was an orange sickly glow.
Fire.
He was shouting, banging and kicking on the cab's doors and windows.
Nothing budged, nothing broke.
And, somewhere in the distance, he swore he heard male laughter.
The last thing he always saw and remembered was the woman's face.

Elizabeth's.

And then, a couple of days ago, he was introduced to her.

The girl of his dreams!

No wonder he was shocked when she stepped out of his nightmare into his reality.

Up until then he had tried to justify it as a meaningless glitch in his brain.

Some random sub conscious thought.

Now he could no longer find any rational explanation.

It was why he was prepared to accept an alternative answer, and why he believed me.

Nevertheless, he told me frankly, if I had 'phoned him yesterday, I wouldn't have made it past the porters' lodge.

But last night everything changed: the dream changed.

The nightmare repeated as before, but this time it didn't end with Elizabeth.

Instead Kevin was suddenly aware someone else was there: standing outside the car.

Someone who opened the door.

So when I rang him this morning his mind was ready and open.

And when he met me later this same day, he told me it was not for the first time.

Of course I was the new addition to his dream!

It gave me the chills.

Until now I had always been the one in charge of the "twilight zone."

Now I understood how the recipients of my "visions" felt.

Sometimes its good to see the other point of view.

Besides I had asked for him to believe me and he did.

The moral being - be careful what you ask for.

So what now?

I could see from Kevin he viewed me as the answer to his prayers.

To him it was obvious: I was cast in the role as some sort of guardian angel.

While I might consider myself many things an angel was not one of them!

I have always thought it strange how quickly the most intelligent modern man reverts to faith or primitive superstition in the face of the unknown.

It may have been different if Kevin came from one of the science disciplines.

He may then still, in my humble opinion, be wasting precious time looking for a logical solution.

But fortunately he was an historian.

In my limited experience a more open minded and liberal breed.

So what do we do?

Well on the basis of 'safety in numbers' and 'three heads are better than two', I make a suggestion - if he is willing.

We contact Elizabeth and arrange to meet later that evening.

I can tell by the silence which follows, this is very last thing he wants to do.

I don't blame him.

There is a lot of common sense in the plan to stay as far away from each other as possible.

But I think we both know what cannot be avoided is better met on our own terms.

So he agrees and we contact Elizabeth.

At 8pm that night we meet up at a local country pub.

We order drinks, as usual I am on my "designated driver" soft option, and we find a cosy secluded spot.

No one really knows how to start.

Fortunately my companions seem to be happy enough in each other's company.

No one, except I, seems to think this an odd development - considering their initial introduction.

Quite honestly as the evening progresses, with no idea of a plan, I am feeling more than a little superfluous to requirements.

Yet another saying springs to mind "two's company."

So at 10.30 pm we take our leave outside in the car park, no further forward and nothing decided.

But two of us are apparently oblivious to that fact.

I ask if they need a lift, but as I do a taxi appears, which they agree to share.

I don't know why they get in - its seems like tempting fate, but they do.

As they do I glance at their driver and it hits me like a wave of nausea, but I don't have the time to be sick.

Suddenly I am in someone else's nightmare.

As the taxi drives off I race to my own vehicle.

I have only one thought in my head.

I cannot let them get away.

Somehow this time luck is on my side.

Their vehicle has been blocked by another cab at the exit.

I follow them out into the deserted lanes.

Keeping the vehicle just in sight, I turn my headlights off.

Not the best or wisest decision, but I can use their tail lights as a guide.

Besides this is a road I have well travelled.

And somehow I know invisibility is important.

I have always been annoyed by films and tv programmes which show a driver being tailed who is completely oblivious to the fact.

Perhaps these people just never use their rear view mirror.

But I couldn't rely on that here.

Fortunately for me the car ahead is keeping well within the speed limit.

So my only concern is the possibility of some unfortunate nocturnal animal running unsuspectingly under my tyres.

Thankfully that doesn't happen, but further up the road something else does.

Just a couple of miles into the journey I remember there is a sharp bend and prepare to brake when I see the red beacons ahead jerk sideways, twist around, and disappear.

At first I am not sure what I am seeing, but then I remember Kevin's dream.

The taxi has turned over.

I pull in a few yards behind where I last saw the lights.

I turn off the engine, and, grabbing a small torch from the glove compartment, jump out the car.

As a force of habit I automatically lock it - I have also seen some of those films before - I never get in a car without checking the back seat!

I know all this seems irrelevant, but it made perfect sense to me at the time.

Besides it only took a few seconds, which were not wasted.

I was already searching for the whereabouts of the taxi.

There it was not far away - down a steep bank.

I could see smoke, but as yet thankfully no fire.

Then I saw something else.

It was all a bit surreal.

A figure was standing next to the overturned vehicle laughing.

It was the taxi driver, and I had seen him before.

He was the reason for my frantic pursuit.

It was the night of the team building exercise, in the hotel car park, as I said goodbye to Elizabeth.

It was her boyfriend, Martin, and then I remembered another conversation to which I had paid little attention at the time.

I was too busy concentrating on her story about Kevin.

But when I saw him masquerading as a taxi driver it all came back.

Elizabeth had said she would have to break it off with him: he was so possessive sometimes it frightened her.

Then I heard screaming and ran towards the vehicle.

My sudden movement grabbed his attention, he turned and stared at me.

As he did so I clearly saw the petrol can he was holding, and pouring over the vehicle.

I had no choice - so I didn't hesitate.

I hit him as hard as I could across the head with a large branch I had picked up from the accident debris.

Not an action I would normally recommend: the possibility of a fatal injury is too risky.

But as I said I had no choice.

It was him or us.

And a fractured skull would be a much kinder death than the one he planned for them.

I don't think he hit the ground before I had flung open the back

door of the taxi, and grabbed the two occupants.
We all cleared the steep bank as though it were no more than an
invalid ramp then paused at the top.
We were looking back at the burning taxi, where I saw a figure
slowly standing up.
I had not killed the would be murderer after all.
I am not sure whether I was happy or sad.
Unsure whether to go and help, or finish him off!
I think we were all debating the same dilemma when the
question was answered for us.
The fire had obviously reached the fuel tank, which triggered an
almighty explosion.
The blast, which blew Martin into purgatory, pushed us
backwards - almost to my car.
By the time we recovered I could hear the fire engine sirens in
the distance.

Later, still a little dazed, I recall having the fleeting hope that I
wasn't going to make an habit of killing people.
Or rather, in some bizarre way, getting people to kill
themselves.
Of course neither was intended.
Both were accidental, both gave the satisfaction of some sort of
poetic justice.

But on the whole if I was going to be an instrument of justice,
I'd prefer to be a Guardian Angel than Nemesis.

# Chapter Fifteen: Good

Nothing comes from nothing.
Nothing ever could.

Strangely enough both believers and non believers alike accept this, although neither can provide any proof.
Probably because it makes sense.
To date no one, no laboratory, has been able to create something from absolutely nothing.
Some argue our very existence proves otherwise, but no one has managed to go back far enough to reach a point where there was nothing.
I am no expert, I'll freely admit, but even the Big Bang Theory seems to rely on the concept of 'something'.
The explosion, or more accurately, expansion of the Universe: and its evolution up until this moment, are based on matter, energy and space.
In other words, an awful lot of something!
OK I can feel I am probably losing you.
So suffice it to say even the BBT provides a good argument for some divine hand, and so presumably a meaning to life.
Unless, of course, we are all at the mercy of some cosmic mad scientist, or cruel puppeteer.
A strong possibility given the state of this planet, and the subject for several books and films
Interestingly though most religions find the BBT completely compatible with the existence of God.
After all what better way to create a planet, a very beautiful planet, than with a spectacular burst of energy.
The only argument is who, or what, created that birth.
This world may be prophesied to end with a whimper, but most scientists and theologians are happy to agree it could have begun with a bang.
I only mention all this because it is not only relevant, but vital to this story - my story.

I cannot prove there is any meaning to our lives, but on the other hand no one seems to be able prove to their own satisfactory - let alone mine - there isn't.

Have you ever considered why so many are so quick to ridicule any sort of supernatural belief?

If it doesn't hurt them and helps others why are they so zealous in their opposition?

Of course they would cite their noble aim is to expose superstition and banish fear.

And so, without realising the irony - drag humanity into the light!

But it doesn't explain their extreme hostility, which borders on phobia.

And in fact that's exactly what it is.

Everyone knows by now that hatred is a well known response to fear.

Fear of something they cannot explain, cannot quantify, and are not prepared to accept: a leap of faith.

Well after the experience with Elizabeth and Kevin, I think I am ready to take at least a small step.

How could I not?

Of course some would argue the whole episode was completely arbitrary, a string of coincidences.

But let's add all those up.

Beginning with Kevin's dream.

Followed by his subsequent meeting with Elizabeth.

Then my meeting with her.

Which in turn led to Martin.

Kevin's second dream the night before my 'phone call.

Opening his mind to my arrival.

Which in turn led to the three of us meeting at the pub.

And afterwards my recognition of Martin

All ending with Kevin's dream being replayed in reality.

And all taking place within a couple weeks!

It was like a very large and complicated jigsaw puzzle where none of the individual pieces made any sense.

That is until all were eventually fitted together to form a perfect pattern.

Perhaps a little too much coincidence?

But even with all this I doubt I could convince any die hard cynic the possibility of any divine invention.

They would bring up the randomness of the whole thing.

Why would God choose to save these two people from all the thousands dying every day?

And it's a valid question: one people have been asking for generations.

Why them, why him, why her, - why not me?

Blind faith seems a bit of a cop out answer.

But, without poisoning your present and future with rage or resentment, there is no other.

Over the next weeks and months I was forced to confront my own role in all this.

In the end I decided to take another small step, and accept what I could not change.

It should be enough, in my own small way, I had helped Elizabeth and Kevin to change their future.

In fact give them one.

I didn't feel any pride in this accomplishment - it wasn't really mine.

Instead, and its not a fashionable word or idea nowadays, I felt humble.

A word which has become forever linked with the repugnant ever so 'umble' Uriah Heep.

Of course Dickens intended it as comic satire, but the mud has stuck.

Perhaps my willingness to accept it was a sign I was evolving - growing up.

I didn't need to feel important, I just needed to do what I was intended to do.

After the dust settled from that shocking night, I continued to see Elizabeth and Kevin for some time.

It wasn't like Joan.

It was something we had all shared and understood - we were the only ones who could.

As far as I know we never imparted any of the details to another soul.
It was easy enough to explain the bare facts to the authorities without any embellishment.
Its all they were probably ready to hear anyway.
Just a simple tale of fanatical jealousy, which happily ended with accidental suicide rather than premeditated murder.
Besides none of us were very enthusiastic about ending up in adjacent padded cells.
Or maybe even worse, sharing the headlines and a lifetime of notoriety in some dubious expose magazine.
A year later we drifted apart.
Well actually I stayed where I was.
It was Elizabeth and Kevin who married and moved to California, where he had been offered promotion in the form of a professorship.
I was a little sad, but not surprised.
I knew it was inevitable from the moment we all met together in the pub.
Call it whatever you like - whatever makes you happy: divine intervention, kismet, or settle for coincidence.
Somehow I knew it was always meant to be.
Perhaps love was even the real reason behind the whole business - not hate.
Love is often underestimated because it is a word devalued from frequent misuse.
But real love is more powerful than hate, because it is about sacrifice not self.
Whoever wrote my favourite quotation from the Bible knew that:

Love is patient, love is kind, it is not envious.
Love does not brag, it is not puffed up.
It is not rude, it is not self serving,
It is not easily angered, or resentful.
It is not glad about injustice,
But rejoices in the truth.

It bears all things, believes all things, hopes all things, endures all things.
Love never ends.
(1 Corinthians:13)

Something comes from something.
Something always does.
But it does not necessarily follow that something bad cannot produce something good.

# Chapter Sixteen:  Evil


Well here I am back in jail again.

A few more hours have passed and I can just see the clock ticking around in the office.

I feel like Gary Cooper in High Noon, and for this apparent reason begin humming the signature tune,  which seems appropriate.

'Do not forsake me oh my darling.'

Around that time I am handed another menu.

Probably to shut me up:  like the rest of my family we may have many gifts,  but singing (or humming) is not one of them.

This time it takes a little longer to bring my order - probably the fast food place is busier now.

While I am waiting I have an unbidden and unpleasant thought: what would I pick for my final meal on earth?

Then another idea occurs to me.

I imagine most Brits on death row don't have the luxury of enjoying - if such a thing is even possible - their last meal.

I doubt any order for fish and chips,  roast beef and Yorkshire pudding, or even a decent curry,  could be fulfilled.

Thank God the food arrives to derail this depressing train of thought.

Southern fried chicken, as the title may give you a clue, is a regional delicacy, and it's one I have come to love.

While that famous chain brand is fine,  and, according to research, one of healthiest takeaways you can eat.

Closely followed, I should add, by good old British fish and chips.

Nevertheless I  was hoping for a home cooked meal - coming from a local family restaurant.

From the plain brown paper bag which was handed to me I was optimistic.

I was not disappointed.

The spicy coated chicken was amazing, without being overwhelming, and the side order of chunky "chips"  was a great improvement on the usual skinny French fries, usually more oil than potato.

Despite the cheap paper plate, and napkins in lieu of cutlery, it was a real gastronomic treat.

Perhaps emphasis on the food rather than its presentation helped.

Like the joy I remember as a child - eating my grandmother's homemade chips in a cone made from yesterday's news.

There was no pudding - my choice.

Although I think the sugar addicted officers were a bit mystified by this, since they kept asking me if I wanted a doughnut.

And it may sound like a stereotype - but I am here to tell you its not!

At least not in that jail, where a box of doughnuts was a permanent feature.

The simple fact is I don't have any sweet teeth, and I have learnt most American desserts and cakes are exactly that.

Whereas most diners "save themselves" for afters, I would always opt for a starter instead.

So satisfied I sat back to digest my lunch and thoughts.

As I said earlier I have come a long way since my grandmother's death.

There's been no great revelation.

I still don't understand the whys and wherefores of my "gift."

To be honest - I no longer care and have given up trying.

It is what it is.

Life's too short to waste, and the older you grow the shorter it gets.

But I had come to terms with the fact that although I couldn't hope to understand the reasoning behind it all, it didn't mean I could ignore it.

So over the years I found myself in some situations where angels would fear to tread.

A few have been a pleasure; many more a pain in the posterior, but none do I regret.

I think, with only one exception, most of the individuals I have met may have been flawed human beings, but humans nonetheless.

Without exception they all had a reason for their behaviour.

Some a little warped - some downright criminal - and always motivated by greed and self interest.

Most a little mad.

But not one of them truly beyond redemption - if I had given them a chance!

Although I may only have been a 'tool' in their demise I cannot help but take some responsibility.

It's how I was brought up.

As I said there was one exception.

One for which I feel absolutely no guilt - and never will.

Only once, thankfully, have I come across an individual who was so vile he made me convinced not only angels, but demons truly walk amongst us.

But then I had never before met that ghoul known as 'the serial killer.'

There is no reasoning to his behaviour, and it is generally a male.

They find it clever and amusing to fool people - who are desperate to believe anything other than the existence of pure evil.

They will say whatever the supposed experts in human behaviour want to hear.

Tales of an abusive father, a dominating mother, bad genes, psychiatric problems,

The list goes on and on.

But it does not include the truth.

They are sadistic psychopaths.

They enjoy inflicting pain and suffering on others, and the only thing usually abnormal about their childhood was torturing dumb animals.

They are predators, cunning beasts who prey on the weak and vulnerable.

Although, because they are "intelligent" human beings, do so not for survival, but for power and pleasure.

As you may gather I am not one of "bleeding hearts" brigade.

At least not when it comes to serial killers!
It was just after the turn of the century,  the new Millennium, when I met mine.
At the time I may have retained some belief in the innate goodness within everyone.
Afterwards the illusion was shattered, and I never made such a mistake again.

It was a hard lesson to learn because it cost an innocent life.

# Chapter Seventeen: Angels

May 2000.
The celebrations were over.
The predicted cyber disaster never materialised, nor any prophesied Armageddon.
The worldwide web was still up and running, while the planet was still spinning round.
As far as I, and most of the world, was concerned nothing had changed except the date.
However quite a lot had happened to me in the period up to that point.
The six short years between the episode of the taxi and this momentous year.
Stories for another time.
None of them anything I had wanted or planned.
Neither something I expected given the unspoken vow of silence we had all taken.
But as Benjamin Franklin said: "Three may keep a secret, if two of them are dead."
I wouldn't blame either Elizabeth or Kevin if they had told anyone the truth behind the story.
After all it began as his dream.
His prophecy - his property.
Besides there were lots of other possible sources and over the years many more.
I had grown up a lot in the meantime, and was now more realistic about my expectations of human beings.
In fact I had grown up to the point that the millennium was a special year for me too.
In October I would reach my half century.
You really only have two options with such a milestone.
You can either ignore it, or celebrate it.
Being a glass half full type of person I decided to do the latter.
So I had arranged a special meal for twenty of my closest friends and two members of my family at The Bear Hotel in

nearby Woodstock.

It had an outstanding reputation for the quality of its food, and the warmth of its welcome.

For others, however, it will forever be linked with the antics of two of its many famous patrons.

Liz Taylor and Richard Burton, who in the 1960s, used it as their country retreat.

The current owners are obviously not averse to the notoriety, and are proud to announce that the original four poster bed is still in room 15.

However, given the nature of the couple's turbulent and passionate liaison, I hope they have changed the mattress!

No rooms booked, or celebrities invited, to my party.

Unless you count my sister and brother who were coming over from America for the occasion.

But this was still over five months away.

Now for me it was the best time of the year.

Spring just before it dies back in summer.

When my garden looks its best, and has the added advantage of requiring little effort.

Thanks to my grandmother's attentions it is a little paradise in the spring.

But, despite my best efforts, it becomes a veritable desert in the summer.

When all the bulbs die back to show bare soil, which either needed replanting, or left to look like the sort of urban wasteland often seen in zombie films.

And a lawn which either requires regular watering or continual mowing.

I simply cannot get summer flowers to survive, let alone grow.

My dearest wish would be the traditional cottage garden, but either the soil or slugs make that impossible.

Besides I find annuals rather sad little plants: living and dying in one season.

It reminds me too much of the frolicking lambs we see in the fields and on Easter cards in April, who never live to see Christmas.

Perhaps they are better off not knowing their fate because neither they nor I can change it.

So from June until September my only concession to the season are roses and some hardy shrubs:   although I have never quite learnt how to prune either.

Sometimes geraniums,  which are perfect for the heat of summer, but have resisted every attempt at propagation, and die with the first frost.

I have come to the conclusion,  while I may have inherited many skills from my grandmother, "green fingers" is not one of them.

My attempts at growing vegetables fare no better, in fact usually worse,  since they produce nothing.

Seeds or sets they just seem to be absorbed back into whatever ground, or tub,  I put them in.

Not even a green shoot.

Slugs again seem to be the main culprits,  and with a small colony of hedgehogs, I refuse to put down pellets.

This year I had decided to make one last ditch attempt at some sort of summer display.

So at the end of May I took myself to a local garden centre, with the intention of finding something which would endure the slugs, soil and me!

As it turned out I found a lot more - and none of it survived.

I wandered around the large store, both enthusiastic and depressed.

Wondering at all the beautiful natural creations,  knowing I would destroy them.

Like someone picking a live lobster for lunch, something else I have never been able to do.

But I eventually pick some plants - from the reduced stand, in the belief that as they were going to die anyway,  I may as well give them a slim chance.

So somehow I have managed to make myself feel good,  instead of guilty.

Having made my selection, I find a till,  and join the short queue.

There's a young woman in front of me,  whose trolley is hidden by all the foliage and blooms.

She glances back at me and at my basket filled with sad stunted little rejects, and smiles.

It's a lovely smile and I know she is one of the rare ones.

Although it is said "the eyes are the windows to the soul," in my experience its completely untrue.

Most people have successfully learnt to hide themselves under a veneer of their choice.

Except to people like me, who have never learnt to trust their eyes rather than their feelings.

This soul will never learn to be devious or see it in others.

She is as trusting as a lamb.

And for some reason it worries me.

A few minutes later, in the car park, I see her loading her small car when a young man approaches her.

He seems to be asking for some help.

She locks her car and goes with him.

For some reason I feel that sudden nausea again.

Why do I dismiss it?

Because what could be more innocuous than a garden centre on a bright and sunny day.

What could be so terrible about a young man, who at this distance looks no more than a boy.

Finally, what God would allow such a sweet soul to walk into harm?

So, to my everlasting regret, I leave with my purchases, which I am convinced will have a short future.

Nevertheless as soon as I get home I give them a good soaking and plant them in containers with the hope this will provide some protection.

By then I'm tired and only half watch some documentary on the t.v.

I go to bed early, and think I have forgotten all the events of the day.

But as soon as I fall asleep I begin to dream.

And it quickly becomes apparent I have not.

I am in a car park which looks suspiciously like the garden

centre.

A young man approaches me.

A young man with a plastered arm and asks if I can lift some plants into his van for him.

He seems likeable and innocent enough, so I go with him.

But as I approach the wing mirror to his vehicle I see my reflection.

I am the young girl at the checkout.

So while everything is telling me to scream and run I keep following him.

Slowly like the nightmare I am in.

There are plants sitting near the rear of a transit and I begin loading them.

Horrified I find myself getting up into the back of the van to do so.

As I stack the last it goes dark.

The doors are shut and I know I am not alone.

I don't have time to make the scream, which is now too late, before I feel a blow to my head.

It is still dark - but there is a little light - coming into my bedroom windows from the street lamp outside.

I give a little gasp of relief as I realise I am home, and sweating like no time since a few years ago when I had chicken pox.

It takes a few moments more for me to fully wake up, and I know I will not be going back.

The bedside clock tells me its almost 4 am, so I get up and make myself a cup of coffee.

Not my usual beverage, but while tea may be the "cup that cheers," coffee is the best antidote to sleep.

I take it into the living room and sit in front of the television, which triggers something.

A memory I wasn't even aware I had.

Last night, exhausted, sitting in front of the "box," and taking its information into my subconscious.

Now I remembered.

The documentary - about Ted Bundy.

So perhaps I could rationalise my nightmare because it made

sense.

The notorious serial killer whose modus operandi was to lure young women into his vehicle with a request for help, and the prop of a plaster cast.

I now suddenly recall an older film about this monster, played appropriately by the personable Mark Harmon.

As I said not all demons come with horns and a tail.

I remembered in this dramatization Bundy also uses the cast as a weapon to subdue his victims.

But my dream was not just a re-enactment of something I had unconsciously seen or remembered last night.

It included something I had witnessed during the day in another car park.

Another young man asking for help with what I now realised seemed to be a broken arm!

So could it simply be a chain of thoughts, a weird twist of fate, and that blasted coincidence again.

Or, it could be a copy cat.

Some pervert who believed that imitation is the most sincere form of flattery.

Whatever it is, I know I have to go back to that car park and now!

I know the complex of shops, which includes the garden centre, is never locked.

So I quickly finish my drink, get dressed and leave.

Even so by now its almost half past five and the light of a new day.

Its not a long drive and, with no traffic, only takes a few minutes.

As I drive past the entrance I see the woman's little car still parked in the same space.

I only notice now it is in a slightly secluded spot away from the main shops.

An attractive area, landscaped with shrubs and trees, probably provided by the garden centre.

It was a busy day yesterday, and all the convenient places close the shops were taken.

The car park is empty, but for some reason I choose in the same spot I previously occupied, and walk over to her car.

I can see from the distance the flowers still crowded into the tiny hatchback.

As I get closer I can see that they are already beginning to wilt: its been a warm spring.

All these thoughts, and many more, pass my mind as I approach.

But none stay except one which is becoming desperate, but I try to stay calm and think rationally.

Trying to rewind the scenario.

Trying to remember where they had both gone.

With the help of my memory, and my nightmare, I manage to follow the path he led her.

And, as I turn the corner into a more heavily planted area, I recognise the place where his van had been parked.

Nothing left except a few shrivelled leaves - from the plants left at the rear of his van.

The remnants of the bait used to lure his victim.

Because now I am convinced, now I know, one "angel" is no longer in this world.

# Chapter Eighteen: Demons

I ring the police.
Having watched, like most of us, probably too many CSI programmes, I am mindful not to approach the scene.
But a little learning can be a dangerous thing, which can make people over confident and a little arrogant.
There may be just the chance of contamination.
Although I doubt it, because murderers also have television sets.
The beauty of technology: it is available to all.
The danger of technology: it is available to all.
And I am convinced any intelligent criminal worth their salt would learn as much about their adversaries as possible.
And, despite his years, I have the feeling this particular monster is clever.
More worryingly because I know it is a lesson in survival gained through experience.
As I wait for the police I think about my "cover" story, which actually is the truth - apart from the dream.
That may be stretching their credulity just a little too far.
Besides, I have other reasons.
Not least, it may distract them from finding the girl.
Although it is too late.
For the first time in my life I know she is dead.
So I tell them what I had witnessed in the car park, followed by the documentary about Bundy.
A strange coincidence, I later made a connection with, and acted upon.
They are convinced.
I must have become a better liar than I thought.
So I watch the police cars and crime scene vans arrive, and see the investigative machinery begin to grind into action.
As I do so, two facts become clear.
They will not find anything to help them.
But I will.

Not that I have any premonition about either.

It is simply that he is too cunning to leave any trace, and this is not his first killing.

He is clearly enjoying the hunt too much to risk getting caught.

This is why I seldom have any sympathy or empathy for the excuse of insanity.

There may be genuine cases, but in my, perhaps harsh, view I believe if someone is crafty enough to avoid justice they are sane enough to know what they are doing is wrong.

And to face the consequences.

The unpleasant truth is they simply love what they do.

So, with no apologies for my unfashionable attitude, all my compassion is reserved for the victim.

The person whose last sight on this earth was the cruelty and pleasure in their murderer's eyes.

But I will find this demon, and have to do so before he selects his next prey.

Unless he already has, in which case the clock is already ticking.

Because, whatever else happens, I will not allow this monster to cut short another precious life.

I will not carry more guilt on my conscience, even if it means I have to pay a heavy price.

So I begin my own investigation.

The scenes of crime experts and detectives are busy around the abandoned car.

They may, or may not, find the site of her abduction.

I told them what I had seen: the point where I had seen them disappear.

They should find the leaves, but may not realise their significance.

They may just conclude they came from the landscaped borders perhaps the result of some disturbance: natural or man made.

But, courtesy of my dream, I have information they don't.

I know where the leaves came from.

So my immediate thought is - where did he get those plants?

The police will, of course, consider the possible evidence of

CCTV.

The thought makes me look up and around.

What I see does not surprise me, given the thoroughness of his preparations.

There are none in the car park, but will they check with the garden centre?

Probably, since it was the last place the girl was seen, apart from the witness - me.

They will check with all the shops because her kidnapper could have visited any of them, or, and my view, none.

But in any case there must have many young men in the busy complex that day.

Because I have another clue which I did not pass on to the police.

The supposedly broken arm.

Why did I omit this piece of information?

I argue the point and convince myself of its logic.

I could not be sure from my view in the car park, and cannot tell them about my dream.

But actually I know the real reason, which I am not yet ready to admit - even to myself.

I don't want the authorities to catch him.

I don't want him to get an opportunity for mercy which he did not give to the girl.

I don't want a version of justice which may risk more lives in the future.

Oddly enough I don't believe in capital punishment, although I often feel as though I would like to administer it!

Human beings are all fallible and the death penalty is an irreversible mistake.

But I do believe in pure evil: heartless and incurable.

Then and there I decided to take a leap of faith.

Abandon any remaining doubt, trust my instinct.

Leave logic for the scientists and justice with an impartial, less corruptible judge.

Whatever higher power guided me, it had never failed me: I had failed it,

I had listened, but not acted, and now someone, a very special and innocent someone, was dead.

Instead I would do the job for which I was intended.

The one I should have done yesterday.

I would catch this bastard.

What I was not prepared to do was sit back and wait for another tragic headline in the newspapers.

So where do I begin?

Well for a start, I will never, ever again, ignore such a feeling.

And I will begin where I ended yesterday: the garden centre.

I can hardly ask them to view their video camera footage - if any even exist.

Garden centres do not have the monetary attraction of banks or jewellers.

Although I am sure it happens.

Another lesson I have learnt: people will steal anything!

But while some may consider armed robbery, I doubt whether most shop lifters would resort to sticking a rubber plant up their jumpers.

In those days expensive security measures were limited to businesses with the most to lose.

But while visual evidence may be unavailable to me.

I can think up some excuse to ask about a young man with a broken arm.

When I go back later the grapevine is already groaning with rumours, delivered with a mixture of relish and relief.

A natural human reaction to the misfortune of others.

Sadly another facet of human nature is the "sticky beak" effect: the store is heaving with customers.

The explanation for my return, if I need one, is simple and obvious - to purchase more plants.

So I rescue some more rejects, and listen to all the excited chatter.

When I get to the checkouts the line is much longer than yesterday.

But the woman on the till is the same.

She immediately recognises me - which is both a good and bad sign.

Good, because she needs no prompting to begin a conversation. Bad, because it connects me to the girl, and could make my next question difficult.

I had already thought up a way to broach the subject which should cause no suspicion.

I'm not even sure what good, or how further forward, the answer will get me, but I feel I need to ask it anyway.

So I wait until there's a pause and then cue my well rehearsed lie:

"Oh by the way I almost forgot - did you see my nephew in here yesterday. I was supposed to meet him in the car park but think I missed him."

She asks "I don't know - what does he look like?"

# Chapter Nineteen:  Hide

She began by shaking her head.
Young men on their own are not the normal clientele of garden centres.
A fact I had anticipated, and something for which I had allowed in my story.
I decided to make him a landscape gardener.
I could see her filtering the events of yesterday,  temporarily setting aside those concerning the young girl, and concentrating on my question.
So far so good.
The next question was hers.
"Oh yes I remember now.  But doesn't his injury get in the way of his job?"
So I had my answer,  but what good would it do?
However she had not yet finished.
"Of course I remember.  Nice polite lad - I've seen him in here a few times recently ."
Which changes everything.
And makes it easy for me to come back with the response.
"Oh good - do you know when he will be back?"
And just in case she later wondered why I couldn't contact him.
" He just moved into the area and I don't have his number or address."
She seemed to accept everything at face value.
Either a very trusting soul or gullible person.
If she thought he was a "nice polite lad" I knew one of two things:   either he was an accomplished performer,  or she had no inbuilt lie detector.
I had yet to meet this paragon of virtue,  who may be the best actor since Olivier.
But,  if my reaction from a distance was so awful,  I was not looking forward a closer encounter.
On the other hand, she had easily believed my own feeble lie.
And she must have found him extremely charming,  because

once her memory had been jogged, she needed no further prompting.

Being memorable is probably not the best characteristic for any criminal, let alone a serial killer,

But attack is the best form of defence, and Ted Bundy was often described as being something more than attractive.

Charismatic.

A quality you do not easily forget.

She hadn't, and went on with further testament to the good character of my 'nephew.'

For such a young man he must be extremely successful, because he was always very busy.

He only came in once a week around the same time on the same day.

The conversation was over.

I paid for my plants and began to leave.

I heard her call after me:

"Give your nephew my best wishes and hope his arm is better soon."

He really had made an impression.

But sadly for her, I didn't think he would be back.

He had got everything he wanted.

Nevertheless I would return next week - I had a valid excuse and he may choose to keep up the charade for a while longer.

A successful mission in more ways than one.

There were no video cameras in the store.

I also had my answer about the origins of the plants.

But it left me with many more questions.

Not least - how did he know she would come in at that particular time on that particular day?

With so many plants she could not be a regular customer, unless she had a large garden to fill.

A fact confirmed by ear wigging on the chattering garden centre staff.

None of whom had ever seen her before.

And they would know because, like my charming "nephew" she was not easily forgotten.

Unlike him she was the genuine article.

So how had he known her movements, and another important question.

Serial killers it is said, and on their own admission, covet with their eyes.

They are attracted to their intended victim by sight.

Where then had he seen her?

Questions which I needed my own plan to answer.

So, like him, I began devising one, which I later called "stalk the stalker."

Everything has its plus and minus side.

To start with the latter: never underestimate your enemy.

In this case a very cunning and manipulative one, and above all dangerously intelligent.

He had not survived so long by charm or luck alone.

He planned his campaign like a five star general, but therein, I trusted, was his Achilles heel.

What I was counting on.

My advantage in this unusual game of 'cat and mouse.'

I was relying on the fact that the cat did not realise he was also a mouse.

He may be concerned about the police, but they would be part of his forward planning.

Tried and tested.

Which had so far kept him free.

His arrogance would keep him focused on the task in hand - and pleasure ahead.

Hopefully not what was coming up behind him.

But first of all I had to find him.

One thing was sure, I couldn't wait until next week.

He may have selected his next victim and, quite literally, have her in his sights.

I had a couple of possible ideas.

The most practical being to follow the 'copy cat' theory.

So what did I know about Ted Bundy.

I recalled some facts I may have subconsciously indigested from the documentary.

But most people, certainly those of my generation, have heard it all before.

Firstly during his arrest and later his execution.

One possible solid lead was his vehicle.

Not the vans, which were usually stolen.

But Ted Bundy was notorious for his distinctive car, ironically one known at the time for a very different reason.

Star of the comedy film "The Love Bug" Herbie was a white Volkswagen beetle.

Bundy's was described as beige.

Quite a common vehicle then, but fortunately it now falls in the category of a rare classic car.

Some research may be worth my time and effort.

The other information I remembered about Bundy was the stuff of nightmares.

Bundy, like many serial killers, had his own hideous 'trophy' collection.

A fact discovered mainly from his own confession, but confirmed by some gruesome police evidence.

He admitted to not only keeping severed heads from at least twelve of his victims, but to dressing their hair and making up their faces!

Thankfully I quickly came to the conclusion, checking the media for any similar mutilated corpses, would be a waste of time.

Why?

Because if this ghoul was faithfully following his mentor's M.O. - there would be no records to search.

Bundy kept most of the bodies well hidden in remote areas, so he could return to, what he considered, his "possessions."

Consequently most were never found.

Although he confessed to thirty murders the actual number is considered to be more than a hundred.

Of course the American serial killer had a much easier task with all the large wildernesses at his disposal, but there are still many remote areas in our own small country.

You only have to look at the "missing persons" statistics to realise how easily someone, or some body, can disappear.

As usual I have a reason - other than morbid sensationalism - to inflict these grisly details upon you.

To make you understand what sort of monster I was dealing with, and why I had no choice in what happened.

So I was left with the possibility of some research into a VW beetle connection, but precious little else.

Even if I could find a registration number - what then?

From all I can gather it is unlawful to share ownership details with members of the public.

And still the question remained: what was the connection between victim and murderer?

Where had he seen her?

All my practical leads seemed to have reached dead ends.

So I was left with my other option, and by this time I was ready for bed.

Perhaps the answer was waiting there.

"To sleep, perchance to dream."

Although of course Hamlet isn't talking about sleep, he is considering death.

Either way I wasn't particularly optimistic about the outcome.

I may have come to accept my abilities, but I am no closer to controlling them.

But perhaps that's the key - don't try to.

Let someone else take control.

Just drift off to sleep and see where it takes me.

Not where I thought!

It would have been unpleasant, but understandable, to have another nightmare about serial killers in general and Ted Bundy in particular.

No, instead I find myself back at the bloody garden centre.

In my dream I decide maybe I should apply for a job.

One way or the other I am spending more time here than at home.

The rest of the night I am chasing around trying to find Brenda - my friendly cashier.

Although strangely I don't recall noticing her name tag.

Somehow though I know this is her name and that I must speak to her.

It's urgent.

It's important: I need to tell her something I forgot.

But in this strange nonsensical neverland I don't remember what it is.

By the time I wake up I am exhausted, frustrated, confused and really, really, irritated.

And left with the feeling I have forgotten something important, and although I don't remember it yet - I have.

Something which could jeopardise my whole plan and ultimately the lives of many others.

But for now I am left with a new problem.

Why should 'Brenda' - if that is her name, be the star of my dream?

And what do I have to tell her?

So much for sleep solving all my problems.

I woke up with even more questions, and not one answer.

The only thing I know is I have to go back - again!

Maybe something there will jog my memory.

For the third time in as many days, I know I must get back to the store.

Perhaps it will be lucky.

As it turns out I don't need the garden centre for inspiration, but I do need to find 'Brenda.'

While I am driving along the well known route, with my mind blank, it comes to me.

I have made a mistake.

Pride comes before a fall.

I am not as clever as I thought I was.

I had been so pleased with myself and my lies, that I never considered one important, and now obvious, possibility.

What if my 'nephew' does return, something I had not considered likely, but don't criminals often return to the scene of their crime?

What if my new friend Brenda tells him his aunt was looking for him.

Then one of two things will happen.

He may be curious and come after me.

I am not his type, but I am a nuisance and a threat.

Not the best scenario, but not the worst.

He may cut his losses, and move on, to continue his career elsewhere in peace.

So I need to fix this and find Brenda.

With this thought I enter the car park - again!

The garden centre is the first store to open, and has only just done so.

Not many cars parked yet - probably employees - but for some reason I drive to the spot where the woman's little car was left abandoned.

From here, for another reason, I walk the few steps which enable me to see where the van was parked.

Of course the van is not there, but another vehicle is.

Yes it is, as you clever people have probably guessed, a cream coloured Volkswagen beetle.

Somehow why am I not surprised?

But I am now even more concerned than I was before.

More desperate to find Brenda.

But while I am rushing over to the garden centre I ask myself: was the dream sent to find her, or him?

As I enter the store I feel as though every hair on my body is on end and every pore a goose bump.

I seem to see everything around me at once.

But I don't see any one.

As yet the tills are vacant.

I move into the building my eyes searching for Brenda.

But also for a pleasant young man, whom at the same time, I both anticipate and dread.

Eventually I see someone - an assistant putting out floral displays - its my friend.

I come up behind her, without speaking.

Like a hunter, or stalker, careful not to alert any one else within earshot.

For I am convinced he is not far away.

But Brenda - and I see her name tag, senses my presence, and turns towards me.

She looks a little surprised - I don't blame her.

But she recovers well and greets me with the comment: "Hello again - can't keep away?"

Then, without waiting for my answer, adds: "Are you still looking for your nephew - I think I saw him in the car park just now."

I feel myself holding my breath while I let her continue: "I tried to get his attention but I don't think he heard me."

She sounds disappointed, but I know its for her, not for me.

I make my thanks and excuses, and leave.

I don't bother explaining any more.

I understand he wouldn't want to speak to her.

As far as he is concerned she is a stranger and he would want it to remain that way.

He doesn't know that I have unwittingly provided him with a character reference, if not an actual alibi.

I go outside and, before I look, I know his car has gone.

He won't be back.

But he has left something behind.

In fact two things, which I noted before I dashed off to the store.

The registration of his car.

Probably useless to me, but will be valuable if I have to resort to the police.

Which I am hoping will be unnecessary, because of the second something.

A small card, easily missed, but not hidden, on the dashboard of his Beetle.

'Edward Brady: HELP: Young People's Crisis line.'

A name, I would put good money on, is not on his birth certificate.

A combination of two of the most notorious serial killers in history is one coincidence too many.

Edward (Ted) Bundy, and Ian Brady, one half of The Moors Murderers.

Two evil monsters on opposite sides of The Pond, but who shared so many perversions.
One being the need to retain power over their victims, and later their families, by refusing to give up their bodies.
A final unrepentant act of control and cruelty.

Ted Bundy infamously said:
"I don't feel guilty for anything. I feel sorry for people who feel guilt."

# Chapter Twenty:  Seek

So I know his name,  or at least his alias.

There was no address on the flyer,  but there was, of course,  a helpline telephone number.

Then I suddenly wish I was a contortionist so I could kick myself.

I totally forgot,  and never checked,  one thing about Bundy - his career.

Most of it was unmemorable.

Sporadic attempts at higher education.

Abandoned forays into psychology and politics:  mixed with little criminal activity.

Nothing new there!

But one thing stood out,  and that's why I wanted to give myself a hard kick up the arse.

He was a counsellor at a crisis centre,   and a surprisingly successful one.

Although given his persuasive charm and apparently soft hypnotic voice,  perhaps not so surprising.

Ironically he was even credited by colleagues as saving several lives.

What a terrible perversion of power:  the ultimate control for someone like Bundy.

The choice over life or death.

Later that evening I was still thinking what to do with this information,  when I picked up the local newspaper.

I had bought it earlier,  with no other intention than bedtime distraction.

How stupid can you get?

The front page headline was accompanied by a photograph of the missing girl, and I realised I am guilty of the same sin I criticised in others.

I was so busy chasing the killer,  I had forgotten his victim.

I needed to find out more about Sara Blake,  so I began by reading the article.

She was just 19 years old.

The bare facts, with a view to eliciting any information, or sightings, were as follows:

Ms Blake disappeared yesterday, in suspicious circumstances, from the car park of the local garden centre.

All this I know - and more.

Probably since I did not give all the details to the police, and, in their turn, the police did not release certain details to the press.

There was no mention of her car being abandoned - but that would count as "suspicious circumstances."

There was mention of a witness - which would be me - but, thankfully, no name.

But I read on, turn to page two, where I find what I am looking for.

The knowledge which will help me know Sara as much as I know her murderer.

And hopefully the combination which will give me the link, and a way forward.

What the media would call 'the human interest' angle.

Sara had recently moved south from her home in Sheffield, where her retired mother and father still lived.

She had just purchased her first home, for which her parents had loaned her the deposit.

The loan being her decision.

She had the old fashioned belief that a parents' financial responsibility ended when their children grew up enough to appreciate money and earn it for themselves.

They were obviously very proud of Sara.

All this was clear from the journalist's words.

But what was hidden was more important to me.

With a birthright which includes paternal Yorkshire grandparents I could read between his lines.

No doubt her parents were themselves too proud to admit the fact that they were obviously struggling financially.

But, as was common in earlier generations, they had saved a little for a rainy day.

They loved their daughter so much they would have been happy to give her all of it.

And Sara loved her Mum and Dad too much to treat them like a bank, or more accurately a bottomless pocket.

So their only child had left home with the intention of moving south to get a better paid job.

A decision which would ease their burden, and not only pay back the loan, but provide support for their rapidly approaching old age.

They would have given her the world if they could.

Which she would have returned, if she had been given the chance.

If some selfish, sadistic son of a bitch had not taken away her life.

I paused.

I was cold - with anger beyond any normal description of the word.

I rarely drink spirits, but I opened the brandy I keep for special occasions and poured myself a triple.

I sat down with it and continued reading.

Her parents apparently were 'concerned' but hopeful she would return safely soon.

I didn't believe a word of it.

Knowing their daughter they were out of their minds with worry and undeserved guilt.

Blame which I intended to put squarely where it belonged.

So I read on.

Already the plants were explained.

She was making a new home.

But someone had known this, someone she had told, someone she knew.

The article said she had not gone to university herself, but now worked in a local college.

Where everyone liked her.

I could believe this, except for that little word 'everyone.'

Although sometimes 'liking' and even 'loving' are more often a cause for violence than hate.

So was the connection at her new job?

The article continued to explain why she was so universally respected.

She was that increasingly rare and wonderful human being: one for whom life was joy which she wanted to share with everyone she met.

She truly wanted to leave this world a better place, without reward or even recognition.

So it was natural for her to take on extra curriculum volunteer work.

A youth crisis line.

Everything suddenly slipped into place.

Now I knew where he had seen his victim, how he knew so much about her, and possibly why he had been waiting for her at the garden centre.

The only question left was 'what was I going to do about it?"

I could take this information to the police - they would probably interview the college and crisis line staff anyway.

But as I said before I didn't want any verdict which involved mercy, however well strained.

He didn't give it to Sara, or her parents.

Deep down in my primitive and savage soul there was a definite satisfaction in the Old Testament type of justice.

Also a permanent, and therefore safer, solution.

Despite this I don't really think I intended to act as some sort of vigilante executioner.

I think I just hoped for the best, or worst, depending on your point of view, and took another leap of faith.

So the final question remained.

How?

# Chapter Twenty One:  Crime

The answer came that night.
Not in a dream,  but after sleepless hours of thought and planning.
Sleep came later - in the early hours.
When I awoke at 10am,  I was refreshed,  hungry enough to eat a hearty breakfast,  and was ready to start.
By now you should realise my fondness for sayings,  so I will give you another:
"Well begun is half done."
First of all I needed to know where he lived.
This was included in my plan and had taken the most time and thought.
Like any criminal the problem is not committing the crime but not to get caught doing it.
But I thought I knew how.
It did involve some personal risk,  but not one which involved the police or prison.
No,  my gamble involved more dangerous stakes.
Because I intended to go into the beast's lair.
The most dangerous animal on this planet,  and had no idea what I would find there.
So how do I find his address?
Actually not as difficult as it appears.
I had two possible leads - the university and the crisis centre,
The crisis centre was too risky, so I opted for the university.
Besides I felt more comfortable there,  with my old picture research connections,  and visits to Dr Lambert.
But I didn't use any of them.
Instead I rang up under the pretence of a national insurance contribution query.
A much safer,  less hazardous, route.
One only leaving a faint trail,  which would soon disappear completely.
Even if the police later asked questions,  no one would be able

to answer them.

As I had guessed from his youth, and confirmed, thanks to an online directory, Edward Brady was not a member of any faculty.

So my enquiry was restricted to the non academic staff.

Eventually, after a few moments on hold, I discovered an interesting fact.

Mr Brady was not a porter, scout or cleaner.

He worked in the maintenance department.

As a part time gardener.

I can't help but smile - so my lies weren't complete fiction after all.

The last piece of the puzzle.

Now I definitely know why he was waiting for Sara at the car park.

From all this I could have found out his address, but I didn't need to.

Luck, fate, or some higher power, was on my side, because the helpful voice at the other end of my temporary 'burner' mobile seemed delighted to provide it.

I just hoped she wouldn't be in trouble when the excrement hit the fan!

And I could guarantee - it would.

But whichever way I thought about it, and believe me I thought about it, there was nothing to link me to any of it.

Perhaps Brenda at the garden centre may just remember the 'nice' boy and his aunt.

But even if she made some sort of connection I had been careful not to leave any evidence behind.

I always paid cash and she never knew my real name, any more than she had known his.

Besides I never intended to go back there again.

Of course there was always the risk of a chance encounter, but I was willing to take it.

I had no alternative.

Now I had everything to commit the perfect crime.

Although at the moment I wasn't quite sure what that crime

would be.

I suppose though I knew, even then, there could be only one outcome.

Once you decide to abandon the legitimate judicial route, your powers increase, but your choices lessen.

I'm not sure what exactly I was thinking.

I suppose I was kidding myself about confronting him and being able to see a speck of humanity still within.

Some possibility for redemption.

But realistically, I knew I was dealing with a dangerous and callous killer, for which there were only two options.

Deal with him, or let him be.

The latter I could not even consider.

Letting him be meant letting other people die.

The former I wasn't sure I would be able to carry out, or live with the consequences.

I was certain about one thing.

If I didn't survive our encounter, neither would he.

Whatever else did or didn't happen: I couldn't let him walk away.

So I left tomorrow's worries for tomorrow - it could worry about itself.

Sufficient for each day its own trouble.

And my trouble today was setting a trap.

A trap which required bait.

There was my problem.

I could not risk involving anyone else, so really there was no problem.

Because there was only one possible candidate.

# Chapter Twenty Two:  Punishment

Of course I was the only choice.

The live bait.

The next question:  how do I set the trap?

The plan I came up with wasn't very complicated,   but sometimes simplicity, like honesty, is the best policy.

Besides there was a certain poetic justice to it.

I liked it because it turned his own scheming against him.

There is always a special satisfaction in the words of Gilbert and Sullivan:  'letting the punishment fit the crime.'

But first of all I need to do some preliminary 'leg work.'

I needed to undertake  a little reconnaissance.

No time like the present.

And I already knew,   from my new garrulous friend at the university,   he was currently working somewhere in the grounds.

So I found one of my old security badges, and dug out some old unused charity envelopes from the hallway drawer.

Neither of which would stand much scrutiny but I wasn't planning to get close to anyone.

So I made my way to his neighbourhood,  which was only a couple of miles away.

I passed the location,  and parked my car in a nearby shopping car park,  and walked back.

It was a quiet street on the edge of the city,  in what once would have been the suburbs.

A long row of detached three storey urban mansions:  built,  I would guess,  when Victoria was on the throne.

One time reserved for the top end of the university:  titled professors and higher level academics.

Most,  I would guess from their sympathetically converted exteriors,  were now multi occupancy.

From the amount of  empty wine,  beer bottles and fast food containers littering the once impressive drives,  I would also guess,  student accommodation.

But best of all - empty.

No cars, or bicycles in evidence.

All residents at their studies - or the pub!

My heart is beginning to sink.

I had hoped, given his 'enthusiasms,' he would be a lone wolf and live alone.

But as I walk closer to my objective I can already see it is not like its neighbours.

It is another large prestigious Victorian villa.

But here there had been no modification, in fact scarcely any maintenance at all.

Unlike its fellows, which no self respecting ghost would remain to haunt, this place would be a perfect location for a gothic horror story.

In fact it probably was.

I can already imagine the interior - the place where I cannot fear to tread.

Neglected, dark and dirty, and an ideal place to spring a trap.

Of course there was no guarantee who would be the hunter, and who would be the prey.

Best not to think too much about that!

But I did wonder how such a young man had managed to afford such a place.

My only thought was an inheritance.

From all I knew of him, he had no nearest or dearest - except of course for an aunt!!

I decided to take a closer look, courtesy of my supposed 'charity' collection badge.

One positive thing about ageing: the older you get the more inconspicuous you become.

Except to people for whom your continued presence is a nuisance and reminder of their own mortality.

And the rarer individuals like Sara, who had been brought up to respect her elders, and value their experience.

On the negative side, this cloak of invisibility eventually leads to the vanishing point of no return.

But now, for me, it was a useful tool.

I went up to the solid front door with its ornate brass knocker, which I tapped and then banged - I could see no bell.
There was no reply, no responding sound, and no movement apparent from inside.
It was what I hoped for, and but hardly dared to expect.
After a few more minutes I had seen all I needed.
Time to go.
I had twenty four hours to wait.
Twenty four hours to go over my plan, and try to catch a few winks.
In fact once I had come to the conclusion: if it's not broken don't try to fix it, I fell into a deep dreamless sleep.
I woke up bright eyed and bushy tailed, and hopefully ready for whatever the day threw at me.
Little did I know it would be a spanner!
Same time,, same disguise, as yesterday, I left home.
A chain is only as strong as its weakest link, which in this case was a ground floor rear window.
I had marked it yesterday.
During my failed attempts to find someone to make a donation!
That would be my story today and I was sticking to it.
Access to the overgrown back garden was easy, via a ramshackle gate.
The window was a two pane sash, and only guarded by the traditional centre catch.
Easily opened by a pocket knife - which I had brought.
It was small, but I was smaller.
So this time I climbed through, not having the slightest inkling of where I was going.
The windows were so dirty nothing was visible from outside.
Imagine my surprise when I switched on my small torch and found myself in a state of the art steel kitchen.
A modern kitchen was acceptable, but as I crept nervously through the rest of the house, I found the same minimalist, almost clinical, vandalism.
All the beautiful original woodwork had been stripped out and replaced by glass and metal.

As you can guess I hated it.

There are places for such modern renovations, but, in my humble opinion, a beautifully hand crafted, turn of last century house is not one of them.

Once I had given myself a quick tour of this sad gutted shell of a building, I am depressed and ready.

I almost wished the exterior had reflected the interior.

This was somehow more unsettling.

It was like a body stripped and mutilated.

I shivered and removed the untraceable mobile from my pocket in order to make its final call when I hear something.

Something beneath me.

It sounds like a faint thud: barely audible.

My objective had been to call the university and lure Brady back home.

Where I had intended to prepare a less than warm welcome.

But perhaps now I didn't need to.

Maybe he was already here.

The one fact I have learnt about making plans: they have to be adaptable.

So I follow the sound back towards the rear of the house.

Where I lose it, but find an original wooden door.

The only one in the building.

Then I realise where this leads.

Of course in such a large period house there would be a cellar and I had found its entrance.

To say that I was anxious was an understatement.

Anyone who has ever watched any horror films knows the two places you never go are the attic and cellar.

Both places where you know danger lurks and a swift escape is impossible.

The moment where everyone in the cinema is silently shouting "don't go down there."

So I could not believe what I did next.

I tried the door knob and amazingly it opened.

To a different world.

A pitch black portal to Hell.

I swore to God I actually smelt sulphur.
The stuff of nightmares.
I fumbled for a light swtich.
There didn't appear to be one.
Probably just as well since I wouldn't have known whether to use it.
Likewise with my torch.
I couldn't risk either until I found the source of the noise.
It could just be what remained of the old house 'breathing.'
Joints moving, pipes gurgling, but I had to be sure.
The stairs down were so dark my eyes had difficulty adjusting, and it took a few moments before I could see there was some light.
Not much, but enough for me to negotiate my way down into the damp stench.
There were other smells too.
A foul stench which I would not care to investigate, but not after all sulphur.
A trick of imagination on the senses.
It again reminded me of every horror film I had ever seen, but one in particular "The Silence of the Lambs."
Then I heard the thud - this time louder, closer.
Again I edged towards the sound.
Thud - what was that.
Then I heard something else - a soft moaning.
Low, but enough to recognise as a young female voice.
Sara?
I searched my pockets for the torch, but it wasn't there.
Damn.
But this didn't make sense: it didn't fit.
Bundy never kept his victims for long - alive.
I carried on into the darkness - following the sounds, and a small sliver of light, which is growing stronger.
I was completely unprepared for what I found - in the twilight cast through a dirty cobwebbed basement window.
A dirty old mattress in a dark corner and someone was lying on it.

It was a young girl, but it wasn't Sara.
She had obviously been beaten, there was dried blood in her hair which had run down her cheeks.
She was unconscious but alive.
As she moaned, she slowly rocked from side to side.
And the heavy shackle which restrained her, thumped against the concrete floor, and echoed around the ceiling and walls.
This altered everything.
My priority changed from retribution to a rescue mission.
But how?
I could not leave her, but could not move her.
Even if the head injury permitted it, I had no way of cutting through the metal.
All this passed through my mind while I was standing there, feeling helpless.
I didn't try to touch her: not knowing what further damage I could cause.
But, I remember a district nurse telling me, while I sat with my dying grandmother, to keep talking to her.
Hearing, scientific evidence tells us, is the last sense to go.
So while I thought, I talked - words of comfort which I hoped sounded more convincing than I felt.
Time was not on our side, and I could see no other choice but to ring the emergency services.
If it's the same detective I met at the car park, then I thought he would act first and ask questions later.
Brady should still be at work for another couple of hours.
They could pick him up there.
Perhaps all was not lost.
So I got out the cheap, but trusty mobile, once more intending to make a call.
Not so reliable after all - there was no signal.
Of course not, in this pit.
So still speaking softly, as much to reassure myself as the girl, I made my way back to the stairs.
I just reached them when I hear another, different, sound.
A door closing: the front door.

Which reminded me -I had left the cellar door open.

An instinctive reaction.

To provide a lifeline - a path of escape.

Now it might be the cause of my death.

Because I knew it was Brady who had returned.

Maybe he had left work early, or never gone.

Another mistake.

Of course I had checked his schedule, but I had not taken into account one possibility.

He could have found a new victim earlier than he, or I, anticipated.

Perhaps the quick response to Sara's abduction, thanks to my intervention, meant he had to dispose of her.

In which case his replacement, the young girl in the cellar, was my fault.

After all the questions and planning, only one was now important.

Did I have time to creep upstairs and close the door?

It was the only option I had, so I began ascending: one quiet step at a time.

For some reason I began counting them.

I had reached the eighteenth, I told you it was a deep basement, when I heard something else.

The worst possible sound in the circumstances.

A voice, and it was very close.

And just a few steps above me - at the top of this stairway between heaven and hell - I saw the light.

It was not bright daylight or the fluorescence of a bulb.

It was the beam of a torch.

My torch?

There are few more terrifying pieces of advice than: "don't look back but run as fast as you can."

Well I couldn't run, but I cautiously began to step backwards.

Not the best procedure, but I did not want to turn my back to whatever was approaching.

His first words had been more of a quietly mumbled thought, but now was a raised audible challenge.

"Come out - there's no where to go."

Brady stepped into the doorway.

I couldn't see his face: the torch was too strong, but I could feel his presence and I was transfixed.

I knew then what the expression 'a deer frozen in the headlights' meant, and how it felt.

He was right, there was no where to run, or hide, even if I reached the bottom of the basement.

It was his territory, his game.

But I continued retracing my steps, if only to try to keep my distance from him.

Instinct once more kicking in.

He began to follow me.

Both of us moved carefully and slowly.

In slow motion: like a bad dream.

At that desperate moment I considered putting up some resistance.

Better, literally, to go down fighting than be caught like a rat in a trap.

But then something strange happened.

In fact several things happened at once.

The light from the torch swung wildly upwards and then disappeared.

At the same time my pursuer shouted.

This time not at me, but an involuntary reaction caused by surprise or shock.

The next thing I knew was something, or someone, pushing past me.

I was hit so hard by the force that I broke through the wooden handrail and fell backwards into the darkness.

I remember once, as a young child, slipping down a rock face while on holiday in Jersey.

This was the same sensation.

Time slowed down and I was acutely aware of everything, especially my own mortality.

I remembered thinking I could not possibly survive this without serious, if not fatal injuries.

But I wasn't afraid.
I wasn't even concerned.
It was best described as 'an out of body experience' while still being in it!
While all this was happening, somewhere beneath I heard a terrible sound.
Like the impact of a soft body on a hard concrete floor, and, in my disconnected state, briefly wondered if it was me.
But it wasn't, because I landed a few seconds later.
Then all was silence.
Despite all the warnings against moving someone after a serious fall.
I slowly sat up.
Convinced that no one could survive such a fall without serious injury I began checking my body.
Beginning with my legs and moving upwards until I reached my head.
Apart from being slightly breathless from landing on my rear ribcage, I was winded but fine.
Although shocked and a little confused.
How had I not only survived such a horrendous fall, but escaped serious injury?
Then I realised I was lying on something soft - a mattress - old and horribly stained.
The cause of my deliverance.
Which I could see through the beam of a torch.
Not mine.
Now I tried to make sense of what had happened.
I picked up the torch and began my investigation.
All the time wary of Brady's whereabouts and the shadows where he might be hiding in wait.
But when I do find him he is in full view - lying at the bottom of the stairs.
He was not quite so lucky as I.
His body looks like a broken puppet - one leg is definitely broken.
Contorted at an unnatural angle, with something white

protruding through his torn trousers.

From the position I would guess his thigh bone, or more correctly his femur.

A nasty compound fracture.

An injury which would normally mean a long unpleasant recovery spent in rods, pins and plaster,

Except for the fact I now notice his head, which is facing at an impossible angle to his body.

Not quite The Exorcist but pretty damn close!

He probably broke his leg on the way down, and the impact with the floor did the same to his neck.

Looking at his shattered remains I have no compassion, no sympathy.

Only the hope, he experienced a few moments of the pain and fear his victims felt, before he descended into Hell.

He will never ever hurt anyone again.

And I had no part in his punishment.

Well - not quite.

Next to his body is another torch - mine.

I couldn't find it when I needed it earlier because I must have dropped it at the top of the stairs.

Which proved to be my salvation and his nemesis.

# Chapter Twenty Three: Kindred

Now, finally, I used the phone - to summon the police and ambulance.

While I waited I used the time to concoct yet another feasible story.

Probably not my best effort given the short notice, or easiest task given my situation.

But I came up with some tale worthy of Hans Christian Anderson.

Maybe I should take up writing fiction instead of picture research.

I quickly realised I couldn't use the charity collection ruse: my props wouldn't stand up to official scrutiny.

So I based it on as much fact as I could.

I had revisited the garden centre - true.

There I had found an advertisement for his gardening services - false.

But I doubted this would be checked.

They would make enquiries at the university, which would connect the appropriate dots.

Besides it was the best I could do.

A subsequent email exchange had led to his address and an appointment.

This might prove my weakest link.

I mean what self respecting, intelligent, serial killer, would invite a complete stranger to their home with a living, breathing victim in the basement?

But murderers are frequently arrogant as well as clever, and, as I said before, ageing brings many advantages.

Who would suspect someone like me?

The rest was easy.

The truth, embroidered with one little lie.

He left me in the living room while going to make us a cup of coffee.

I heard the noise and go to investigate.

The rest, as they say, is history.

The only thing I need to do, is go into the kitchen and boil a kettle.

I had the time because I knew where it was - my point of entry into the premises.

At the same time it gave me the opportunity to put the catch back in place.

So I did exactly that - being careful to use a paper towel as a fingerprint protector - which I then put into my pocket.

I just had time for one thought before I heard the approaching sirens.

I hoped no one asks me to turn out my pockets.

It would be hard to explain a torch and pen knife.

The police were the first to arrive.

They found me back in the cellar, softly speaking to the girl while gently holding her hand.

The paramedics arrived shortly afterwards and took over care of the patient.

So far no one had asked me anything.

Someone, a policewoman I think, took me upstairs and sat me down in the living room.

Usual procedure I would imagine: keep civilians out of the way while the professionals get to work.

Little bit late for that.

Then, to my amazement, she offered me a cup of tea.

Of course I refused - I don't want to contaminate my carefully placed evidence - or get her in trouble for doing so.

She left the room, and I was beginning to think, everyone had forgotten me.

Until the door opened again and there stood my old 'friend' the detective from the car park.

He introduced himself again - Detective Inspector Colin Thompson.

Although I had not forgotten him.

And for all the right reasons.

You can find kindred spirits in the most unlikely places and people.

He gently told me that, thanks to my swift actions, the girl would be fine and hopefully not remember much of her ordeal.

He also told me the killer did not have time to dispose of Sara - again thanks to me.

Her body was found, wrapped in a blanket, in another corner of the cellar.

What he did not say, but we both knew, was the significance of this to her parents.

They would be able to give her a Christian burial.

They knew where she was, and had somewhere to grieve.

They had been spared a lifetime of misery.

A blessing denied to so many whose children's bodies have never been recovered.

Never laid to rest.

They would never forget, but they could try move on.

The monster may have murdered their daughter, but he had no more power over her, or her parents.

He had not won.

Now I am prepared to give my account.

But incredibly Detective Inspector Thompson stands up and leaves the room with the request to call in the police station tomorrow to give my statement.

Perhaps he is playing with me, or perhaps he is giving me the opportunity to get my story straight.

As I said you find kindred spirits in the strangest places.

So the next day I go down to the police station and dictate my tale to the duty sergeant.

Which I then sign, and so becomes the crime of perjury rather than a simple lie.

Everyone seems happy and no one appears suspicious.

Then, on my way out, I see a familiar figure standing in the doorway.

He thanks me and shakes my hand, but he has nothing to say to me.

On the other hand, I have something to say to him, and as he

walks outside with me,  I tell him.
"When you visit New York next September,  don't take your
family to the World Trade Center".
I don't know where this comes from.
No dream.
No premonition.
Some thought which came into my head - without thinking.
But I hope he listens,  because somehow I know its important.
I think he will.

This will not be the last time I hear from Detective Inspector
Colin Thompson.

# Chapter Twenty Four:  Spirits

It's now around 4pm in my cell.

Afternoon tea time.
But I know I won't be offered any sandwiches (crust less or otherwise),  cakes,  but maybe perhaps some tea.
The cream part of the tea I could live without,  but now the thought really makes me want sandwiches - cheese and cucumber.
Strange I rarely partake of the meal we English call 'afternoon tea,'
Not to be confused with 'high tea.' which is a more substantial formal meal served at table in the early evening.
No 'afternoon tea' is a much more relaxed affair taking place on easy chairs and sofas around a low table.
It has the same historical aristocratic origins as the "sandwich" which itself now forms a major part of the ritual.
The sandwich was created almost a hundred years earlier in the mid 1700s.
When its namesake - the Earl of Sandwich being a notorious gambler refused to leave his card game and requested something to eat at the table.
The cook,  probably cursing with irritation,  apparently slapped a steak of roast beef between two wedges of bread.
An invention which was such a social success it remains one of the most popular snacks.
But afternoon tea does not immortalise the name of its creator:
The Duchess of Bedford.
Almost a century later,  in the early 1800s Anne,  the seventh Duchess,  became so hungry waiting for her 8pm dinner that she ordered tea,  bread, butter and cakes to be served in her room.
A deviation which no doubt again caused a few expletives from her inconvenienced kitchen domestics.
But once more proved such a sensible and sociable solution,  she would later invite friends to join her.

So yet another tradition was born out of need and common sense.

The latter I remember being referred to in the film 'Elizabeth' as a very English virtue.

For once I have no reason, or excuse, for this educational diversion .

But I hope you enjoyed the detour.

Anyway suffice it to say, once you are denied something it becomes irresistible - an obsession.

I am still fantasising about cheese and cucumber sandwiches, when my menu arrives.

In the hands of my favourite gaoler.

A cheery friendly African American man, who treats me as an equal rather than a criminal.

Ironic really since I would imagine he hasn't always been extended the same courtesy.

I cannot say I do not notice race - in fact I just have!

But it really makes no difference to me.

As you should know by now - I don't judge by exterior appearances.

And the only vibes I have picked up from this warden are all good.

So he waits patiently while I check out the menu.

No cheese and cucumber sandwiches available, so I opt for a close modern substitute.

A generic "Subway," in which for convenience, I always request "the full Monty."

Of course I don't say that here - it would lead to confusion and a lengthy explanation.

So I just ask for roast chicken with "the works."

He takes my order with a smile and the remark "good choice."

It may not be my most practical decision.

It arrives oozing ingredients, but it is delicious.

And, with thanks to my 'waiter,' it comes with the tea I requested - no china but a paper cup.

Besides I don't have a sofa or coffee table either.

I probably wouldn't enjoy it so much if I did.

Instead I sit cross legged on the bed, which cannot be harmed by a few bits of salad, or drips of mayonnaise.

Afterwards, I sip the tea, which is hot and passable, with a slight bouquet of cardboard.

My mind wanders off again.

Still no visitor yet and it quiet now.

During all the hours of my incarceration I have never really felt anything about this cell.

Good or bad.

Yet there must have been many former inmates.

Many who have now passed on, in the ultimate sense.

I wonder why there are no spirits trapped in this cell.

Perhaps there are, but they don't want to talk to me, and I certainly don't want to talk to them.

Sometimes though you don't get a choice.

The first time that happened to me was two years after Brady met his fitting and timely end in the cellar.

Up until that point I had never seen a spirit.

At least I don't think so, because when it did happen I didn't realise at first it was a ghost.

You may wonder why, with my sensitivities, I would fail to recognise a dead person.

But then again so many dead people don't realise they are deceased either!

Besides I was not looking for them.

In fact I was actively avoiding them.

Ever since an unfortunate teenage experience with an homemade Ouija board.

Some work mates had created it with a few slips of paper, a pen and a glass.

It began as a lunchtime diversion in the canteen, and ended with my vow never to put myself in that position again

It may be all rubbish, but it didn't look that way when the glass began moving.

I refused to be part of the circle, but was too fascinated to walk away.

So I stood by the door - near an escape route - and watched.

They asked all the usual, mostly self obsessed questions: "Will so and so ask me out?" "will I be rich?"

I remember thinking: if I was a spirit I would be pretty peed off!

You wait all these years to make contact and then you get these morons just asking you stupid questions.

The whole business lost any interest for me, so I left.

I had walked halfway down the corridor when I heard my name shouted.

I looked back and saw one of my colleagues running towards me.

I could see she was excited, so much so, she didn't wait until she reached me to explain

"It wants you."

Now these words fall into the "don't look back but start running" category, in terms of putting the fear of God into you.

I had no alternative but to return with her.

My reception was unnerving.

Everyone around the table was now silent, and turned to look at me as I entered.

All of them, without discussion, shuffled around the table and made a spare place - obviously intended for me.

With the objective of getting this over with, I placed my finger on the upturned glass and waited.

Nothing happened and then I heard a whisper.

"Ask it what it wants?"

So I did.

And the glass began to move.

Now, bearing in mind I was the only person still touching it, this was not a pleasant sensation.

Even worse, in the silence it was the only thing making a sound: a horrible squealing of glass on metal.

Everyone was holding their breath, as it spelt out its request:

"Tell them to leave me alone."

The conversation quickly ended.

The temporary 'spirit' board was dismantled and placed in the bin.

It was never mentioned.

No one ever again spent their lunch time in anything other than eating and harmless conversation.

Later that evening, when I related the story to my grandmother, was the only time I have seen her truly angry.

She was madder than a wet hen.

But not at me.

I think it was the shock of this, as much as the Ouija experience, which made me determined never to mess with anything like that again.

But occasionally you have no choice.

Phantoms are like demons.

You cannot always control their appearance.

They turn up, unannounced, like unexpected guests, and often out stay their welcome.

Sometimes they don't want to leave until they have got what they came for.

The problem, I was soon to discover, is that it is not always clear what they are looking for.

Even to themselves.

Neither do they always arrive in white gowns with rattling chains.

When mine turned up she was wearing a sweatshirt, jeans and trainers.

Perhaps some excuse for my ignorance.

It was June 2002.

Over two years had passed since my last meeting with DI Thompson.

None of the circumstances surrounding our meeting was forgotten, but was safely stored somewhere in my mind.

I had never returned to the garden centre

So imagine my surprise when one day on a bus returning from town, I saw Brenda.

She was standing in the queue at a stop.

Obviously she was not going my way, which was a relief.

She was still in the queue as we drove away, and looking straight at me, which was a worry.

But I consoled myself with the fact it was a temporary glitch in the normal smooth running of my life.

Until I saw her the next day in the same spot.

And the next day.

Each time she did the same unnerving thing.

As I have said several times before: I don't believe in coincidence.

So what was this about?

Had she recognised me, but was her brain taking its time to decide what to do about it.

It rattled me so much I even considered abandoning the research I was currently doing at the central library.

In fact I did change my routine, to avoid the same bus.

But on the fourth day she was still there - waiting to get on.

This time she wasn't waiting.

She was pushing her way onto the bus, and making straight towards me.

In some ways it was a relief - get the confrontation over with.

But as she sat down next to me I realised exactly what was going on.

At such close proximity I couldn't ignore what was now obvious.

Brenda no longer worked at the garden centre.

In fact she no longer worked anywhere.

Some time in the past two years she had retired - from life.

The person now sitting next to me was not a person at all.

At least not in this world.

No wonder no one objected to her rudeness boarding the bus.

Because to them she simply was not there.

Maybe, for some, her presence was registered as a light breeze as she brushed past.

So this is how the anonymity of ageing ends - complete invisibility!

Don't laugh or scoff dear readers.

As they are now, so I - and you - shall be.

My fears about possible recognition and reprisal vanished, replaced by other concerns.

First of all the hope no one would sit on top of her!
Not sure I could cope with that scenario without some sort of emotional reaction.
Horror, shock, laughter, hysteria - probably all four.
None of it acceptable social behaviour for a lone passenger on the no.10 bus - well any bus really.
While I was considering this Brenda began to speak, which in itself created an extremely bizarre situation.
It wasn't the sort of spiritual encounter we have come to expect from a ghost.
But, perhaps we have all taken the menacing phantoms in "A Christmas Carol" too literally.
No, it was as if she were sitting next to me as a living and breathing person -chatting.
In fact she even began with the remark "Hello, how are you?"
Honestly, what do you say to that?
I think I mumbled some standard response: acutely aware of the fellow travellers around me.
Fortunately none were too close.
In moments like these that famous British reserve has its benefits.
If anyone heard they were polite enough not to show it.
I think I even added "And how are you?"
I cannot think of any remark more pointless, or less appropriate to have made.
But the habits of a lifetime are hard to break!
And so it began.
Somehow between her talking, and me grunting we made a pretty reasonable effort at conversation.
It turned out she had been killed in a car accident just two weeks ago.
Since then she had been 'floating around' (her words) trying to find someone to listen to her.
When she saw me on the bus - she knew I had also seen her.
Now all the business with 'my nephew' made sense.
She had seen his photograph in the newspaper headlines, but the police hadn't contacted her, and she saw no point in

contacting them.

At the time she thought his aunt probably had enough to deal with.

Now we were 'face to face' and she was no longer looking through a dark glass, she understood.

Finally, when we are almost at my stop, she gets to the crux of our meeting.

She needs help.

I respond with the usual assumption she wants to move on and doesn't know how to.

I am no expert, but I have seen enough paranormal films and documentaries to know about the theory.

But before I can give any well meaning, but ill conceived, advice Brenda interrupts with:

"Bugger the light - I know where that is, but I have to do something first."

# Chapter Twenty Five: Lost

I am left with the thought - does Heaven know what's coming to it?

But the one definite thing I have learnt.

Ours not to reason why.

Brenda might be a blunt woman, but she was a good one, and deserved her place.

Even if she wasn't quite ready to go there yet.

My stop arrives and we get off the bus together.

No doubt leaving the remaining passengers - and possibly driver - shaking their heads.

Poor woman, obviously lost her marbles.

I don't care: I will probably only see them again  - if ever - on the bus.

In which case they may possibly wonder why I have suddenly found my marbles.

Another wonderful benefit of growing older.

The longer you live,  the less you care about the trivial.

So we walked, and she talked.

She wanted to go on,  of course she did:  so many of her nearest and dearest were waiting for her.

But she had unfinished business,  which left undone would affect the living.

Or at least one.

Her daughter.

Jennifer.

Strange I had never heard her mentioned before, but perhaps with all the other distractions,  I hadn't been listening.

Then it turns out I was right.

She hadn't mentioned her daughter because she had been adopted at birth.

But unlike my own mother,  it had been more than a biological connection.

She had never forgotten her and,  although she knew she had done the right thing,  she had never abandoned her responsibilities.

It was the old story.

A young girl, an unplanned pregnancy, and an older man who disappeared as soon as he heard the 'happy' news.

Men, it seems to me, are so much luckier.

They have the best of both worlds, and, if they choose, everything in between.

They can either completely disclaim all responsibilities and take off.

Continue with their life carrying, maybe a little judgement, but no emotional, or often financial commitment.

Perhaps, even worse, they remain to exert control over the mother and child.

In some cases providing plenty of misery, without much practical support.

A few decide that fatherhood is a matter of choice - theirs.

Something which they can pick up and put down when it suits them.

Of course many boys, and their mothers, would argue 'it takes two,' while at the same time, placing most of the blame on the girl.

My response would be to agree as far as the conception goes, but afterwards the female has little choice.

She can either terminate the pregnancy and be judged as a murderer or unnatural monster.

She can decide to keep the child and carry the stigma (and there is still plenty) of being a single mother.

Or she can opt for adoption.

For most women - and girls - none of these decisions are taken lightly.

I say all this not to make a point - although of course I am - but so you can understand how much I respected Brenda for her decision.

While I am on the subject.

The pro life lobby, always intrigues me.

I may be wrong, and am ready to admit it.

But it seems to me their cause is often plagued by on an "holierthan -thou" attitude: which can be shockingly violent and judgemental in their treatment of others.

Perhaps, instead of invoking their own version of religion, they would do better to remember the Christian advice "Judge not, lest thee be judged." (Matthew 7:1)

In my view you are not qualified to do so until you have "walked a mile in their bodies."

Or, at least, tried to imagine what such a journey would be like.

Still, as I said earlier, imagination, and its companion, empathy, seem to be rare qualities nowadays.

Too inconvenient, too uncomfortable.

But I had done so with Brenda, as I had done with my own mother.

So I could appreciate neither decision was easy.

Although probably more so for one, than the other!

As with my own case, for Brenda there was a similar happy solution.

A childless aunt and uncle agreed to raise the child as their own, with only one stipulation.

She must never know.

And she never did, although as she grew up she was always aware of the kindness and generosity of an older cousin.

The agreement was kept.

All through Jennifer's childhood.

Then, through the preparations for her wedding.

Where Brenda took a back seat, but insisted on paying half the costs.

Followed, far too soon afterwards, by the tragic premature death of the son-in-law she could never acknowledge.

A kind and gentle young man who, with the optimism of youth, had provided his wife with two lovely babies, but neglected life insurance.

She provided two broad shoulders to cry upon, along with anonymous financial support for her two grandchildren.

The pact still held a few years later, when Alzheimer's claimed the minds and lives of her aunt and uncle.

Brenda never married or had any children.

A subject for pity from those who were not party to the deception, and a source of anxiety for those who were.

They need not have worried.

Brenda never broke her silence.

She watched her own funeral, and subsequent cremation, with the satisfaction of seeing her daughter, and grandchildren, take their rightful place in the front row.

Her own parents had predeceased her, so there were precious few family mourners.

In fact only four people sat there.

Although, she was pleased to note, friends more than made up the numbers.

A modest woman, Brenda would not take any personal credit for this sincere tribute of respect and love.

The fourth person sharing the front pew was her younger brother, Nigel.

Fortunately there was such an age gap between the two, he wasn't party to her pregnancy, or the subsequent arrangement.

If he had been, it wouldn't have remained a secret for long.

Because, in his sister's words: "he is a thoroughly nasty piece of work."

While I wouldn't necessarily advocate corporal punishment: Nigel was the product of a 'spare the rod and spoil the child' upbringing.

Sadly, as is sometimes the case with a late child, especially the dearly longed for, son and heir, he had been overindulged since birth.

Whatever virtues he may have been born with, had been pushed aside by one vice: greed.

And this was the issue behind Brenda's concern.

Because as the closest family member Nigel would now inherit his sister's property.

She had already watched as he squandered his half of the legacy provided by their parents' deaths.

Her own estate was not insubstantial.

She had always worked hard and enjoyed few luxuries.

But she had bought a house, which she used any spare cash to turn into a home.

Even so she would not have begrudged him any of it - except for one thing - one person.

Jennifer.

When her parents died she realised the importance of her own will.

So she had made one, in which she had left a small bequest to Nigel: with her daughter being the main beneficiary.

Oddly enough that will had now gone missing.

She had made it quickly, one of those DIY kits - perfectly legal if completed correctly.

And Brenda had taken legal advice to ensure it would be.

She found two friends to act as signatory witnesses, who did not know, or need to know, its contents.

The executor she named as Jennifer, a perfectly natural and understandable action, given her brother's history with financial matters.

Of course 'her niece' knew the reason for Nigel's exclusion from the process , but was completely unaware of his almost complete exclusion from the will.

So everything was signed and sealed.

Brenda told me she had placed the original in a small fireproof box at her house.

The copy she had given to Jennifer, to be opened in the event of her death.

The original had disappeared from the security box shortly after her death.

The copy, her brother had subsequently asked for, and received, from Jennifer shortly before her funeral.

She knew where both wills were now.

Or more accurately where they were not.

She had watched, helplessly, as Nigel burnt them.

She was a little annoyed with her daughter, but she was more angry at herself.

Jennifer seemed to have casually given up the copy, and with it her inheritance.

But at some point, during a time when she had loaned her brother the key to her house, he had got a duplicate cut.

He had probably already seen her will prior to her death.

In fact she could pinpoint a moment when his attitude had changed towards her.

About six months ago, when his moods would swing between overly affectionate and outright hostile.

Obviously he could not keep up the pretence too long.

Brenda was under no illusions about her brother.

Sometime between her death and funeral, when others presumed him suffering from sibling grief, he had returned to her home and stolen the will.

Her fault again.

She had bought the fireproof box for exactly that reason, not against theft.

The contents were after all only valuable to her.

Or so she thought.

Stupidly, she realised with hindsight, she kept the key in the lock!

All she could do was watch as he grinned, while he opened the box, and removed the her will.

This was my mission, if I chose to accept it.

Just another pointless comment - how could I refuse?

But, with all copies of the will now destroyed and lost, how would I start?

As matters now stood there was nothing to stop Nigel from claiming his sister's entire estate.

No doubt blowing it the same way he had done to his parents' bequest.

In the eyes of the law he was the legitimate next of kin.

And we all know the law is not always just.

Brenda did tell me one thing.

While there was no evidence left of her wishes after death, there was proof of Jennifer's birth.

In his haste to remove the will Nigel had overlooked another document.

Amongst all her most precious possessions was a birth

certificate - the only thing she retained of her daughter.

If I could find it, then I could set everything right.

Unlike Brenda and her family I had taken no oath of silence, and could see no harm now in letting Jennifer know the truth.

Easy enough to say, but how could I get to it?

I had no keys to the house.

If indeed the box still remained there.

We knew mercenary Nigel had a set, but I had no chance of stealing those back.

So that just left Brenda's own.

The last time she saw those was when she locked the door on the night of the accident.

Without knowing she would never use them again.

They had been in her handbag.

So the question was 'who had them now.'

Brenda had been too shocked, understandably, at the time to notice.

She was more concerned with her body, which she was horrified to see was mangled and beyond repair.

It was obvious she could not return to that unsustainable shell, but she had not yet come to terms with her new reality.

She was in that twilight zone where she wasn't even sure if she was dreaming.

So she watched as a doctor on the scene, pronounced life extinct and recorded her time of death.

She followed her remains with the ambulance to the hospital, and later into the morgue.

All the while hoping she would wake up.

Of course when this didn't happen, and the pathologist prepared the body for an autopsy, she gave up.

Apparently, she wandered around for a bit.

Lost, confused and little angry.

So when the light appeared, with no other options, she was just about to go into it, when she remembered.

There was someone she needed to say goodbye to, and it wasn't her selfish brother.

As I said she was a good woman, but not strongly religious, so she wasn't convinced about an afterlife.

Perhaps all this was just the final throes of a dying brain.

And, having been denied motherhood for most of her life, she wanted to see her daughter one last time.

So, in her own words, off she went.

Being a sensible soul, and not yet used to this new freedom, she caught the no. 5 bus!

She did briefly consider a taxi, but wasn't sure how to accomplish this.

Of course she couldn't pay for either, but when she stepped onto the bus platform, she instinctively looked for her bag.

That was the first time she missed it.

But she didn't consider it for long: it was part of her other life, no longer needed.

So she just carried on with her journey.

When she arrived, she was faced with another new dilemma.

Why was everything so hard in her brave new world!

How would she ring the door bell?

So she just stood and waited.

While she was doing so, she saw a familiar figure approaching the house.

Someone who obviously could not see her, since he was focussed on the door.

Nigel.

What was he doing here?

I suppose, Brenda thought, he could be calling in for tea and sympathy.

Nigel was an expert at putting on an act for appearances' sake.

But she was under no illusion about his real feelings.

All centred around the question: 'what was in it for him?"

She wasn't wrong.

The front door was opened, and Brenda took the opportunity to follow her brother inside.

Jennifer herself had answered the door, and her mother's heart split between happiness and misery when she saw her.

Brenda would have loved to see her grandchildren: William, a strapping eight year boy, and Samantha, a petite but strong minded, seven year old girl.

But both were at school.

Good timing, and no doubt perfectly planned.

There were no witnesses when Nigel requested the copy of his sister's will.

The reason he gave was plausible: the original was missing and the solicitors needed to verify its authenticity.

I was beginning to wonder if any of us ever tell the complete truth!

Besides what reason would he have for lying?

As far as anyone knew, the inheritance would be his by right anyway.

With the request he return it as soon as possible, and his promise to do so, he was off.

He had got what he wanted.

No tea and precious little sympathy.

And through all this disgusting farce Brenda was forced to keep quiet.

No point in staying with her daughter - she could come back later.

For now she needed to follow Nigel and see what he was up to. Although she was fairly sure she knew.

He went back home - to the small flat he rented with all that remained of his parents legacy.

With no garden at his disposal, she watched as he disconnected the smoke alarm, took out both copies of her will and burnt them in the sink.

Helpless she couldn't even muster enough physical strength to blow out the match.

# Chapter Twenty Six: Found

That was the moment she began looking for help and where
better to find people than a bus.
Enter myself - a very unlikely answer to a prayer.

So we had reached the point where only an old birth certificate
remained, and the keys to unlock it.
Brenda and I may not have much to work with, but we formed a
very unusual, but formidable, partnership.
In our separate ways we had skills the other lacked.
She was able to see things I could not, and I could ask questions
she could not.
Between the two of us within a very short time, and a few more
white lies on my part, we had discovered the whereabouts of
her handbag.
Ironically it was Jennifer herself who now possessed it.
She was the one person who had turned up at the hospital, and
for the staff it was a matter of courtesy and common sense to
give the possessions to a relative who actually cared.
Now I only have to approach Jennifer and get the keys!
Which I did,
After Brenda and I had woven a very tangled web, involving an
old friendship and a promise to return a document, kept for me
in her 'safe.'
Our only hope - it was so convoluted Jennifer would not be able
to follow its thread.
I called about the same time of day as Nigel, with the same
intention: her children would be at school.
Children are wonderful little miniature adults, except for one
thing.
It takes a while for them to learn to fill the gap between their
minds and their mouths.
So, if they smelled a rat, or in this instance a tall tale, they
would announce it to the whole world.
But, as it happened, it didn't matter.

When I met Jennifer everything changed.

She was so much like her mother, I wondered why no one had commented on this before.

Although other people often only see what we want them to see, or what they want to see.

As soon as she saw me, she smiled, which made the resemblance even stronger.

I asked the question: "Jennifer?"

To which she nodded, and continued smiling.

Just as I was preparing to go into my spiel, she interrupted me with the words: "You know only my mother called me Jennifer."

For a moment I am completely nonplussed because I didn't know what her aunt and uncle called her.

The only person I do know, who only ever used her full name, was the person who gave it to her - Brenda.

Who, at this moment, is standing at my side.

Then it dawns on me.

Jennifer knows.

I don't know when, or how, but she knows.

She invites me in, and over a pot of tea with a tin of biscuits, tells me her story.

The main point being: she has already opened the box and, incredibly, has the original will!

As the executor of the estate she took her job very seriously. Besides she never really trusted her uncle.

So as soon as she left the hospital, she went straight to the house.

Although heartbroken at the sudden and unexpected loss, she somehow knew she should take possession of the any valuables as quickly as possible.

Among those she found the security box, so she removed this, along with the small pieces of jewellery her 'aunt' had bequeathed to Samantha.

It was the last time she would use that word.

That evening she was overwhelmed by such a terrible feeling of grief, as a distraction she decided to look through the box.

The jewellery was beautiful, but only interesting to Jennifer as a personal link to its owner.

Like her mother Jennifer simply wasn't bothered by material possessions.

But she was interested in knowing more about the relative who had meant so much to her.

She took out the envelope containing the will, and set it aside. It had nothing to do with her.

The next thing she picked up was an envelope with the words 'Birth certificate.'

She opened it with the thought it related to Brenda and was interested, although not obsessed, about family history.

As she read through the entries, and realisation dawned, she was maybe a little surprised but not shocked.

There had always been something special about their relationship, and now she knew what it was.

Not all children feel a strong connection to their biological parent, I certainly didn't.

Everything alive requires some effort to survive.

It was Brenda who had created and cherished their bond.

Of course Jennifer still loved and respected her aunt and uncle - even more so now.

Since she realised their devotion had been born out of love, not necessity, or obligation.

But she also understood the source of the overwhelming loss she felt.

This knowledge changed everything.

Above all the fact she felt she should read the will - her mother's last testament.

When she did she was torn.

Unwilling to go against the wishes of her mother, yet unhappy to accept them.

Even though the chief beneficiary would be her avaricious Uncle Nigel.

At least their relationship had not changed!

She argued she had been left enough monies from by her adoptive parents.

Which should have been more, but the family home had been sold to pay for nursing home care.

Her current accommodation being a pleasant enough, but exorbitantly expensive, rental property.

Now it became clear why Brenda had suggested moving the small family in with her, and been disappointed when she refused.

Whatever she did, or did not do, with the will, she could not destroy it.

Like the birth certificate it was personal to her.

Her mother's first and last wishes.

So she placed both safely together in a small lockable metal box, kept for special documents and letters.

With her own family birth certificates.

She put her executor's copy of the will in the empty envelope, and replaced it in the security box.

The next day she returned it to Brenda's house - after doing one more little job.

On the way she stopped off at the local library and took a photocopy.

Just in case.

This was the document she had later handed to Nigel.

He never even noticed the difference.

My immediate thought was: wait until he finds out.

When the original will miraculously arises from the ashes.

I would love to be a fly on that particular wall!

Brenda is now sitting next to her daughter on the sofa.

Speechless with pleasure and pride.

Pleasure her daughter now knows the truth, and pride that Jennifer is much wiser than she thought.

She really didn't need our help after all.

So, if we are not here for justice, what are we here for?

Although neither of us say anything: I think we both know.

To put things right and say goodbye.

But how?

Brenda cannot speak to her, and is becoming so used to her new state, she doesn't even try.

She just looks so terribly sad and helpless.

Then I come up with an idea.

It's a bit risky, but the only one I have.

I am not some medium, like Whoopi Goldberg in Ghost, who can channel spirits through my body.

For some mercies we should be eternally grateful!

So I make a decision to reverse an old promise.

With the argument that everything contains a potential for good and evil.

Of course some things are more balanced on one side than the other.

Most people believe 'spirit boards' are dangerous and are tools of the devil.

They are not wrong, but perhaps, just this once, it may be right.

For too long this pair have put other people before, and between, them.

This is their last chance in this life to put it right.

It wasn't ideal, but it was a way they could talk without someone else in the middle.

Sensitive as I may be, I could not do justice to their feelings with my translations.

So I make my suggestion to Jennifer, who, I am happy to say, is rightly concerned about the idea, but agrees.

With the help of a notepad and pen, I put together the necessities.

All this done and in place, I move into the kitchen to let mother and daughter speak to each other alone.

From where I stand I can watch, keep guard, and be available if the need arises!

After my last experience, all those years ago, I am taking no chances.

Although I content myself with the knowledge there is a far better guardian angel to these proceedings.

It is Brenda, herself, who is in control and will, as always, protect her daughter from harm.

Wherever it comes from.

This world or the next.

Most of the time I try to look away.

It is all too intrusive for an eavesdropper, even a sympathetic one.

Although I cannot actually hear a word.

Just inaudible whispers.

The look on their faces is enough for me.

So full of so many emotions.

Its too personal, too uncomfortable.

Then at some point the voices are raised a little, and I catch a few words.

Enough for me to understand they are discussing the will.

It doesn't last long, and it becomes clear from their body language Brenda has won the argument.

It was a forgone conclusion.

How could Jennifer deny her mother this last request, when all her life she had asked for so little?

Besides while she may dispute her own need for help, she cannot deprive her children.

Certainly not in favour of Uncle Nigel.

So obviously all matters are now resolved.

Eventually to the satisfaction of everyone - except aforesaid uncle.

So, all in all, a good result!

Nothing left now but goodbyes.

When I venture another look I see the most poignant sight.

A mother trying to provide comfort to a child with a hug neither can feel.

Or can they - what do I know?

Even after all these years - I have to admit - very little.

Afterwards I dismantle the makeshift board and take away the remnants.

I even remove the glass.

The paper I will burn.

The glass will be disinfected and, erring on the side of caution, then dipped in holy water

The disinfectant is easy - the holy water a little more

problematic!

Although I am still uncertain about the method, I cannot fail to be pleased with the result.

We have to wait just a little longer - for Brenda to see her grandchildren.

Time to go.

We say our goodbyes on the doorstep, while the children are chattering inside.

Jennifer has asked us to stay until she has closed the front door.

It reminds me of all those soldiers who left home asking their loved ones not to come to the station.

But, before she does, she quietly asks me if I can see her mother.

I say "yes: she is standing next to you."

At the same time I see Brenda softly brush back her daughter's hair and kiss her on the cheek.

I don't need to say a thing: I can see she feels it.

She smiles and whispers "I love you Mum."

She doesn't hear the reply - so I repeat it:

"God bless you Jennifer - have a wonderful life and see you later."

All too much for me.

Too many memories of the last moments with my own grandmother.

The door closes behind us and we walk away, deep in our private thoughts.

In silence.

We get as far as the bus stop, where we make our own goodbyes.

As I get onto the bus Brenda mouths the words "thank you," and I wave as I watch her drift out of sight.

From the corner of my eye I see a couple of elderly ladies watching me and whispering to each other.

I can't blame them.

There was no one else at the bus stop.

But neither do I care.

Those days have long gone.

# Chapter Twenty Seven :   The Devil

Its almost evening again.

The officers are getting ready to pack up for the night, and I hope they haven't forgotten their solitary prisoner.
Or the fact that my time,  one way or the other,  must be almost up.
I was not anticipating another night in this miserable cell.
Then my friend comes in and I know, at least, he hasn't.
He greets me with a smile and the offer of a drink.
I am happy to accept both.
Smiles around here are few and far between, and liquid refreshment essential.
I remember once a stay in hospital where I was being continually harassed to 'drink more fluids.'
I know I do not drink enough.
Its always been a problem,  but since working from home, I frequently go for hours without stopping to make, or even pour one.
Sometimes I think my kidneys must wonder if I have died!
Before he goes off to fetch my 'order' he asks if I need anything else.
Like more food.
I decline,  but tell him I am grateful for his kindness.
Then I receive something even more rare:  his name.
He introduces himself as Officer Williams  -  Martin Williams.
No guesses where his Christian name came from.
I imagine he is in his early forties.
He must have been born around the time Martin Luther King, Jr, was murdered.
When he returns he also brings some news - whether its welcome or not remains to be seen.
But it does mean I won't have to spend another night in this cell at least.
Although it does have one advantage.

Here I am special, the only occupant.

If I am transferred to a large state facility, to await trial, then I will be one of the herd.

I am not anti social, but I am a private person.

Until now the implications of sharing a cell, and life, with several strangers had not occurred to me.

Or perhaps it had: I just didn't want to consider it.

Anyway Officer Williams' news will change everything, for better or worse.

Because I have a visitor: the one I have been expecting for almost three days.

The one who will decide my fate, and whether I deserve to be here or not.

I know I do.

So I cannot complain.

Whatever happens now I truly have no regrets.

It was a risk I took, and decision I made, months ago back in England.

To be exact, about six months ago, just after this year, 2010, had been welcomed in.

Though not by me.

By the time 'auld lang syne' was sung: to the accompaniment of fireworks, I would be wrapped up in bed.

When I was younger it was different.

Since their respective marriages my grandmother and her siblings created a new family tradition.

Hers was a large Edwardian brood.

Two brothers and four sisters.

Although for most of her life my grandmother was not part of it, having been brought up by her grandmother.

Which seems to be another family tradition!

But one of the moments they did share was Christmas.

Every Christmas Eve all the siblings, with their own families, would walk to Uncle Jack's house, the eldest brother, where they would begin the celebrations.

Christmas Day was reserved for home, with the occasional

visitor popping in for mince pies and sherry.

But on Boxing Day the festivities resumed, when everyone would meet up again.

This time at the home of Uncle Norman - always known as 'Nin' the youngest brother.

A break followed for everyone to digest three days' worth of food and prepare for the final event.

New Year's Eve.

When a party was held at my grandparents' home.

It began mid afternoon with tea, and ended a little after midnight with beer and buffet, comprised of sausages rolls and sandwiches.

Afterwards all the neighbours left their private parties and formed a conga line - weaving and staggering all around the street.

It is a tradition no longer upheld.

Most of my grandmother's family, one way or the other, have moved on.

Even if they hadn't, the world has changed.

Most people are so busy in the pursuit of a better life, they forget to enjoy the one they already have.

It is a society where neighbours seldom see each other - let alone speak.

Sometimes, in rare moments of happiness or hardship, a community will come back together.

But sadly, in my experience, it rarely lasts.

As soon as the celebration or crisis, is over, everyone resumes their individual path.

So as New Year's Eve became New Year's Day, I was tucked up in bed, blissfully unaware that at the beginning of April my own path would converge with another's.

I didn't really know this person, but I had met her briefly a long time ago.

Sixteen years to be precise.

She was the close family friend in whose care I had left Margaret.

As I said I never heard from Margaret again once she left to find her daughter.

But this year I did hear about her, and what I heard has brought me to this place.

Easter Sunday that year fell on 4th April, and I had planned to take a long weekend break to Bath.

The journey, with the development of a new dual carriageway, was now even shorter, if less dramatic.

The road down into Bath was previously a more exciting introduction to that famous city.

But now the emergency run offs, if you miss the hair pin bends, are all gone.

It has been levelled off, and you now arrive at the bottom without really feeling the steep descent at all.

It may be safer, but somehow it lacks the sense of adventure which for previous centuries must have been part of the experience.

However, for me in this instance, it would be welcome to minimise travel and maximise relaxation.

I thought I didn't know anyone there, now Margaret had gone, and in a way I was right.

I didn't really know Emma, but she was about to put that right. Although she was as unaware of that as I was.

When I arrived and booked into a central hotel my only thought was to rekindle a relationship.

Not with a person, but a city.

Unlike Jane Austen who, apparently could not write there, but described it cynically in two later books, Persuasion and Northanger Abbey, I love it.

But then I am not being forced to stay here, and it is no longer the magnet for the fashionable and pretentious society it was then.

Small wonder if the quiet country woman hated it, although the only proof of this seems to be in her books.

Besides, it could be argued, while the author may not like the bustle and noise of a city, it provided her with plenty of material and inspiration for the future.

But for me, with no prejudice against it, Bath is fascinating, beautiful and full of atmosphere.

In an age when most cities have driven out all their ghosts, Bath has somehow managed to retain its unique spirit.

It has always incorporated the change brought by invaders: whether they were Roman soldiers or Regency socialites.

But essentially it has never changed.

So, as Jane Austen concedes in Emma: "One half of the world cannot understand the pleasures of the other."

And I was on pleasure bound.

The first day I went back over my own old haunts: all the classic tourist places.

Some were nostalgic pilgrimages: remembered moments shared with my grandmother.

I began at the beginning with the Roman Baths, when the settlement was known as Aquae Sulis.

On my departure I stopped at the Pump Room and moved into Regency Bath with a pot of tea and a traditional Bath bun, served with lashings of butter.

Now I should explain these local delicacies are not the normal tea cake variety.

They are their larger, plate filling, cousins.

So much so, often only half the bun is served - in this case I had the full article.

Not to worry - I would be walking it off.

The afternoon was spent exploring all the wonderful, and free, reminders of its Georgian past.

The Royal Crescent and Circus forming the most famous public architecture.

The Assembly Rooms completed the tour where I was happy to pay admission to see the rooms, used as backdrops in Austen books and films, and the Fashion Museum.

I completed the day with yet another huge sweet bun served at the famous Sally Lunn's eating house.

As I said before I really do not have a sweet tooth, but when in Rome.

The unofficial Bath Tourism tour is now over.

The second day, with no plan, I decided to wander off the

normal path to revisit places less generally known but more personal.

As it turned out one of these included the pub I remembered from Joan's funeral.

It was lunchtime, and if the food was half as good now as it was then, what better place to refresh and regroup.

Whatever else I may have been prepared for, it was not renewing old acquaintances.

I don't know what led us both to that pub, on that day, at that time, but I was no sooner in the door than I saw Emma.

I remembered her name because it was forever associated with Jane Austen, and so Bath.

She was at the bar ordering lunch, when I joined her.

There was no reason not to.

We were both obviously hungry.

We had left on good terms, at a bad time.

Both concerned for our mutual friend, Margaret.

So what could have been more natural, once we had each given our orders and sat down together, than the conversation turned to her.

Apparently, it was a subject which had been worrying Emma a lot recently.

When she saw me, it was like an answer to a prayer - again.

It was not a reaction I sought, or even wanted, but I was getting used to.

Unlike myself she had kept in touch with her friend over the past fifteen plus years.

This had ended six months ago.

Suddenly she could no longer contact Margaret.

Or at least receive a reply.

The only source of her contact: emails, had dried up.

Nothing.

She even went back to the old tried and tested - but lengthy - and aptly named 'snail mail.'

She waited and waited.

Still nothing.

Not even her original envelope marked 'return to sender.'

It was like everything she sent was swallowed up into some black hole.

In the meantime she had tried to find any contact for the daughter, Debbie.

Being the reason for her self inflicted deportation, Debbie had always been the main topic of conversation.

So Emma knew quite a bit about her subsequent life.

Or, up until this moment, thought she did.

Now unpleasant thoughts, previously suppressed, began surfacing.

What did she really know, what had she ever really known about the situation in Virginia.

The postal address given, and where she had sent Christmas cards.

As for the emails - well, they could have gone anywhere in the world.

Perhaps there was a way of tracing these, but technology defeated her, and maybe, deep down, she didn't really want to know.

Her suspicions began within a few months of her friend's departure.

Suddenly the telephone lifeline was severed.

Margaret explained in her emails that there were difficulties with signals.

She lived in the mountains where mobile communication was non existent.

Landlines apparently were no better.

Emma didn't know much about such technicalities, and accepted - grudgingly - the explanations.

Besides it was an undeniable fact:   telephone calls were exorbitantly expensive.

So, she allowed herself to be persuaded, emails would be the best substitute.

Afterwards it felt as if she was corresponding with a stranger.

Hard to be otherwise when personal contact is denied.

Words may be powerful tools, but they can also be useful weapons.

So when she had been told about something called 'skype' she was excited.

She would not only be able to resume their verbal conversations, but actually see her old friend once more.

Unfortunately this was easily vetoed - again something about signal strength and wi fi.

Yet this had never previously affected their exchange of emails! Then the belated thought occurred to her:

If a signal was available for an online computer, why not for a mobile 'phone?

So she asked the same technophile who had told her about skype, and got her answer.

She now felt so stupid, and also bloody angry.

She had been taken for a fool, and had happily accepted that role.

With every other avenue blocked the emails resumed.

But as time went on she came to accept the fact: their formerly close relationship was slipping farther away.

Finally, a few months ago, even that ended.

To her everlasting regret she ignored all the warning signs, but worse her feelings.

Something, I have known for a long time, is always a bad move.

But she consoled herself with the thought: what could she do about it?

All this she told me over lunch.

The more I listened, the more worried I became, and the more convinced I was this was not an accidental meeting.

I don't mean Emma engineered it - but someone did.

So the only question remaining was:

"What was I going to do about it?"

# Chapter Twenty Eight: Deep Blue Sea

Well I did the one thing I could.

As soon as I got back from my 'dream break,' which was swiftly turning my worst nightmare, I began a different kind of research.
I am not an expert on the computer, or honestly, much bothered by most of its capabilities.
But, thanks to my publishing job, I knew quite a lot about its potential for fact finding.
I soon found the truth about one piece of information - the address in Virginia.
It was a dead end.
The address itself, a complete fabrication - which led absolutely nowhere.
As far as I could find out, surprise, surprise, it didn't, and never had, existed.
Though in turn, it did provide me with another clue.
This second lead proved more useful.
Craig's surname.
I may be wrong, and despite my abilities, often have been, but I just felt he wasn't far away from his fake address.
So I began searching online directories and social media sites for Mr Craig Wurley.
Thankfully not the most common name, and one I thought he would still be using.
It was what was in his passport and the name he had given Debbie at their marriage.
Besides why would he change it?
If he had any nefarious activities, before or since his time in the UK, he would invent an alias for them.
Incredibly, and not what I hoped or expected, I found him quite quickly.
Actually I was right.

The address I found was just over the border - one state away in North Carolina.

And as serendipity would have it - not too far away from where my half sister lived.

I could kill two birds with one stone.

So I told Emma of my plans to visit my family and look up Margaret.

Which made her happy, and me nervous.

I also promised to keep in touch.

Somehow I didn't think there would be any signal or wi fi problems.

There are mountains in North Carolina.

In fact some very famous ones: The Blue Ridge and the Great Smokey ranges.

But both my sister and Craig's homes were in the east, between the mountains and the sea.

Or more accurately the Atlantic Ocean.

So I booked a passage to cross this on the Queen Mary 2 leaving in early June.

Not the coolest time of the year, but not the most miserably humid either.

Of course at the time I didn't know how long this 'holiday' would last, or where I would be spending part of it.

I had just two months to finalise my travel arrangements and make my plans.

Over the years my dislike of flying has become worse, almost now reaching the point of phobia.

But if it was a problem or inconvenience to others, it wasn't for me.

It has given me so much more than it has taken away.

So although I had some mixed feelings about my visit to America, I had none about the voyage.

How could I?

Seven nights of complete relaxation and pampering!

But enticing as that sounds, it wasn't the reason for my happy anticipation.

For me it was the opportunity to escape from all the worries of the world, in fact the world itself.

If you really cannot live without your daily fix of trouble, strife and financial reports, a ship's newspaper is always available.

In fact one is delivered to every stateroom.

Mine goes straight into the nearest recycling bin.

What is the worst that can happen?

If the sea we are sailing on, decides to explode, or implode - what I am going to do about it?

Personally, though, I tend to agree with T S Eliot:

"This is the way the world ends. Not with a bang, but a whimper."

So until that happens, I am going to make the most of whatever time is left.

For many fellow guests that seems to involve eating as much as possible, as often as possible, whenever possible!

I once heard a master of the QE2 say: "you embark as a passenger and disembark as excess baggage."

Sadly that is all too true.

Particularly so on the transAtlantic crossing where there are no diversions, or exercise, in the form of shore excursions.

And no escape from the temptation of endless food.

Of course there are all the normal good resolutions and initial reconnoitres to the ship's gyms and swimming pools.

Which is usually the only time such facilities are busy!

I know better than to make promises for my body my mind will not keep.

I always pack a swimming costume - and do actually use it: once or twice.

People often ask if I am bored.

I can truthfully reply- never.

While I may not always like humanity as a whole, I love watching people.

It is a strange fact that out of a complement of over 2,500 passengers there are perhaps only a maximum of a dozen you see regularly.

Perhaps it's a question of shared routines, or maybe they are just the ones you notice - or more worryingly, the ones who notice you.

Most of the time it's a friendly mutual greeting, but just occasionally it becomes something you seek to avoid - or worse, dread.

Such an event happened on this crossing.

All the first night formalities were completed: life boat drill, meeting my stewards and dinner companions.

I was settling down to a few days of rest and recuperation, before the chaos of New York appeared through the Hudson mist.

Instead I got more problems.

Or at least one, in the form of a fellow passenger.

It wasn't even as if this new acquaintance was obnoxious or, in many ways worse, a whinger.

And believe me, on my travels, I have met many who have fallen into that category.

One I remember in particular who told me on first acquaintance that I reminded him of a celebrity.

OK, you would think, a fairly innocent, even complementary, opening.

Except he didn't have in mind anyone famous like Elizabeth Taylor, or even Cilla Black.

Instead he chose someone infamous like the moors murderer Myra Hindley.

In fact it was exactly Myra Hindley.

Obviously he had never read the book: "How to Win Friends and Influence People."

Bad enough, but for the rest of the voyage he would greet me by shouting the words "Hello Myra" at me.

Unfortunately usually in one of the large public rooms, and always when it was packed with spectators.

Now such things can give you a complex.

Even though everyone assured me I bore no resemblance whatsoever to that notorious serial killer, it began to put a damper on the trip.

It left me with only two options: to show my offence, or laugh it off.

I was dealing with a middle aged moron, with the mentality of an eight year bully.

I knew any complaints would only serve to increase the problem and the teasing.

So I chose the latter.

No so, one of my other new acquaintances.

Stan, was a British immigration officer, travelling on the ship in order to expedite paperwork, and avoid delays in Southampton.

We were sharing a drink in the ballroom when I received the usual loud bellow of recognition.

When I explained, Stan was so disgusted, he threatened to punch him on the nose!

Ah - If wishes were horses beggars would ride.

Stan was a bluff Yorkshire man, but he was sensible enough not to risk his career for an idiot.

However from that moment the harassment ceased.

On the rare occasions when I saw my tormentor, he quickly turned on his heels.

I concluded that dear Stan issued his own sort of 'restraining order.'

Anyway I hope this proved an entertaining digression on the perils of the sea.

This time it was a completely different kettle of fish!

Sorry - just trying to lighten the mood.

Because the next part of my story is neither amusing nor annoying.

It is in fact quite tragic.

My first night onboard, and I was getting some exercise and fresh air, prior to retiring to the air conditioning of my inside stateroom.

In my view the only drawback to the lower priced accommodation I had chosen.

But who needs a balcony in the North Atlantic?

Except for fresh air, and soon there would probably be too much of that to leave the door open anyway!

So I was taking my final look at England.

Evident now only by pinpricks of light from windows and street lamps in small villages and towns as we steam past Dorset, Devon and Cornwall.

I briefly wondered if anyone was awake out there and watching us.

Our final parting with land would be around 3am at the Bishops Rock Lighthouse, four miles west of the Scilly Isles.

But I wouldn't be sitting up to try and spot it.

By now I was feeling comfortably mellow - possibly the result of my brandy nightcap.

I was also beginning to remember that wonderful feeling of detachment.

Somewhere out there: becoming more and more remote, was the modern world's version of reality,

Where every person is the centre of their own universe.

Out here, on this sea which comprises almost three quarters of planet earth, is reality.

A place where human beings play just a tiny part.

But somehow this sense of your own insignificance is not at all frightening, it is strangely comforting.

At that moment I knew exactly how every voyager setting off into the great unknown had felt.

Yes, nowadays we have all the modern technology to help us circumnavigate the seas and oceans.

And we know there is no edge of the world waiting to swallow our little ship of souls.

But what lies beneath is almost as mysterious to us as it was to the Vikings and Phoenicians.

OK I'll admit this is all a bit dramatic and philosophical for a bedtime story.

It could have been the brandy.

But having experienced the same emotions before, without the alcohol, I knew it was something more.

It was an understanding that I was, at the same time, both important and unimportant.

And happy to accept it.

All this may seem to be irrelevant, but it does go to show my state of mind.

Whatever happened in the future I was content.

All these thoughts passed through my head within a few minutes, while I was leaning on the ship's rail, savouring the experience.

As I finally turned to leave I noticed a figure copying me just a few yards away.

It was an elderly lady - I would place in her late eighties.

She was obviously old, but had been brought up in an age when deportment mattered.

I couldn't see any of her erect body, which was well wrapped against the increasing wind as the ship picked up speed.

Her face was just a little visible - quite white in the light cast from the deck lights.

As is normal with people sharing such self imposed isolation, we began to talk.

I don't remember now who spoke first.

It was obvious we were both British, because our first comments concerned the weather.

The conversation didn't last long.

She seemed a little distracted.

Perhaps this was her first trip and she was experiencing the same feelings as myself.

So I said 'goodnight' and left her to her thoughts.

That night I dropped off to sleep as soon as my head hit the pillow.

But I thought about my deck companion quite a lot during the next day.

Everyone was busy settling into their new routine, their new reality.

Some were obviously having a problem adjusting.

They were the ones who rushed around filling their hours as much as possible.

Others were happy to enjoy the change of pace; did almost nothing, except eat, chat and perch on various chairs around the ship.

The final category, including myself, fell between the two

extremes.

Equally enjoying the leisure, and the opportunities offered on board for, as the brochure says, 'enrichment.'

Lectures and activities designed to inform and educate.

I chose a talk given about George Mallory by his descendant - Penny - who put a very convincing case for him being the first person to reach the summit of Everest.

Well at least the first westerner.

One poignant piece of evidence supported this, or rather the lack of it.

When his body was found seventy five years after he disappeared on the mountain, it was missing one important item.

The photograph of his wife which he had promised to leave it on the summit.

A fascinating and moving story well worth the effort of walking down to the theatre.

Otherwise a quiet day, followed by an excellent dinner shared with good company.

My evening routine is exactly that - the same every night.

Whatever the show is offering - for choice one of the itinerant comedians or entertainers who cruise the maritime circuit.

My night would often end with a visit to the cinema - as long as it doesn't include animals.

Not that I dislike our four legged friends - in fact just the opposite.

After a traumatic childhood experience with 'Bambi' I avoid such emotional draining films.

Although with most other films I have surprisingly eclectic tastes.

I even remember on one transAtlantic crossing watching 'Titanic' in a cinema with standing room only.

Unlike airline passengers, ship passengers are hardy souls, which nothing much seems to deter.

Certainly not when it comes to eating!

So, all in all, a good day with just my evening constitutional to complete it.

My friend was waiting - as I knew she would be.

Don't worry I am not going to inflict my entire trip upon you, like some blogger oblivious to your actual interest, or boredom levels.

But this day, and the remaining five, ended in the same way, with the same company.

And over that short time I found out quite a lot about her.

The first thing, which I knew from the beginning: she wasn't like any other passenger.

She didn't have a stateroom - she didn't need one.

Yes, you're right - she was a ghost.

Although she didn't tell me the first night - in fact she didn't really tell me at all.

I obviously surprised her as much as she surprised me.

If I wasn't the first person to see her, I was the first to acknowledge her.

As the voyage progressed, so did her story.

She had been a passenger on a previous crossing.

Several years ago now.

She had fallen overboard somewhere off the coast of Newfoundland.

People assumed she had killed herself because she had been making a pilgrimage.

Her father had died on the Titanic.

Like him, her body had never been recovered.

But it wasn't that she wanted to put right, and kept her trapped on this ship.

Because of the unusual circumstances it was believed she had jumped overboard.

Her death was recorded as 'accidental,' but widely considered to be suicide.

It was this she wanted to put right.

There was no stigma against this in the afterlife, but she couldn't move on because it wasn't the truth.

I understood that.

But I wasn't sure what I could do about it.

The second night, Mary, for that was her name, told me.

Apparently I had not been the first to see her.

There was someone else on this ship who had, and more than once.

He was one of the ship's senior officers.

Not only had he seen her, but he recognised her.

Because, all those years ago, when he was a junior, he was on duty when he saw her fall.

It was he who had raised the alarm.

She didn't blame him for her death.

To all intents and purposes she was dead as soon as she went over the side.

Between the time it would take to turn the ship, and the frozen waters of the Atlantic it would be too late - even if they found her.

No, the reason for her grievance was nothing to do with what he failed to do at the time.

It was what he had allowed to happen since.

At the time there were no cameras covering that area of the deck, so he was the only witness.

While the subsequent inquest brought in a verdict of accidental death, it didn't quash the rumours.

So Mary found him guilty by omission.

Admittedly it was dark and the man couldn't be sure what he saw - hence the verdict.

But, because his silence, the 'no smoke without fire' brigade had had full rein.

Perhaps if he thought it was self inflicted it would lesser some of his guilt.

She knew it wasn't his fault, but neither was it hers.

She just wanted him to do, which she knew was not easy, to speak up and tell the truth.

Because, in his heart of hearts, he knew she had not climbed the rail and jumped.

I never asked her what she did all day, or why she seemed tied to this spot.

Somehow it seemed rude and irrelevant.

I knew what I needed to know.

Over the years, every night, she continued to walk the decks which had been her last place on earth.

She told me, she could have left.

She knew he could have.

As a senior officer he would have been welcomed by a rival company, or even transferred to another ship.

But somehow they both seemed bound together.

Neither quite sure how much longer this could go on, until I appeared.

It took me another day and night to find and approach him.

It proved easier than expected.

The next night was the Captain's cocktail party - something I usually avoid.

It's a manic event - passengers lined up in their finery to be announced, introduced, and photographed shaking hands with the long suffering ship's master.

I will tell you, every captain should win an academy award for their acting.

I don't think they miss my absence one bit.

But this time I had a different reason to attend.

Because apart from the captain, every other senior officer is expected to run the gauntlet.

I had every hope my target would be there.

And indeed he was.

But it is one thing see him, or even meet him, and quite another to broach the subject.

Most professionals, for obvious reasons, do not want to admit any belief in the supernatural.

I was trusting in all my previous experiences and Mr Macawber's words: 'something would turn up.'

I was not disappointed.

During the socialising period between introductions and the captain's speech I managed to infiltrate his group and strike up a conversation.

Only a brief chat, with a seemingly innocent comment about how so many ships have ghosts.

But enough for him to seek me out after the party and ask if I would have dinner with him in the Officers' Wardroom.

Now I know it wasn't my overwhelming beauty or charming personality which prompted this invitation.

So I temporarily abandoned my place in the restaurant and went with him.

Probably leaving behind a few raised eyebrows.

I didn't care.

As I said before: at my age you cannot afford to waste time and effort giving a damn!

Once in the officers' private dining room, I found myself - by luck or judgement - seated at a table for two.

There were only a few other patrons.

Most of the officers would be hosting tables in the main restaurants.

It was probably an excellent meal, but I don't think either of us noticed.

Because even before the appetisers arrived we were deep in conversation.

There wasn't much small talk.

By the time desserts arrived the atmosphere had changed.

And, if such a thing is possible in so short a time, Ships Services Engineer Tom Robinson and I had become good friends.

He revealed he had avoided the open decks at night, but that night he joined me.

When we began it was just the two of us.

Shortly afterwards Mary joined us, or rather we joined her, and I stood back and left the two of them alone.

It seemed they had a lot to talk about, because I sheltered from the strong winds against the bulkhead, for a long time.

Finally they seemed to pause, and I was astonished to see a fourth join our party.

It was a young man in formal attire, but different from our modern comfortable dinner jackets.

Of course it dawned on me - it was Mary's father.

She looked back at me: gave a smile and wave.

Within seconds just two of us were standing on an otherwise

deserted deck once more.

We didn't speak at all on the way back inside.

We only spoke a little over a brandy in the nearest bar.

But I understood some agreement had been reached about putting things right.

Mary never expected, or wanted an apology, she just needed recognition.

The truth.

Tom was a good man, who had been trapped in a difficult situation.

I knew he would do the right thing.

Peace was long overdue for both of them.

They could now move on.

I saw Tom, in passing, a few more times during my final days on the ship before she docked in Brooklyn.

As for Mary.

Well, suffice it to say, the remainder of my nightly promenades were solitary and undisturbed affairs.

# Chapter Twenty Nine:   Trial

Well at least I managed to salvage part of my intended break.

The ship sailed under the Verrazzano Narrows Bridge just after dawn.
As usual the decks were packed with eager passengers for the event.
They had nothing else to do.
All their luggage was gone:  stacked ready for unloading to the pier.
Breakfast was in full swing,  but not urgent since disembarkation would only take place once all baggage was ready for the customs officers.
Most of the photographers were on the port side,  cameras aimed at the nearby Statue of Liberty.
The other focal point was no longer there.
In the place of the World Trade Center,  was one single building currently in construction.
It was a strange and eerie experience:  the first time I had been back since the terrorist attack.
Next year would be the 10th anniversary.
It seemed like yesterday.
They say everyone always remembers where they were when John Fitzgerald Kennedy was murdered.
Actually I don't,  but I do remember 9/11.
I was with a neighbour sharing our usual afternoon cup of tea, and watching the portable television screen behind her.
At first I thought it was a disaster movie,  until the commentator told me otherwise.
My first thought was my family in US,  who often made shopping trips to the Big Apple.
My second thought was DI Thompson and the warning I had given him.
My only consolation that awful day:  everyone I knew was OK.
My family were safe in North Carolina.

Colin Thompson rang me later in the evening, UK time, to thank me.

He never asked me how I had known, and never did.

We were all in a state of shock.

It was already warm that morning in New York, but I shivered.

After all the times passing, and photographing, those famous monuments to man's genius.

Now an empty space, which was probably the most fitting tribute to man's stupidity.

The new One World Trade Center would rise like a phoenix from the ashes.

It was right that it should.

But, whether or not, I ever came back, this is what I would remember.

A blue sky, with the sun rising higher as our planet moved around it.

And the certainty it would do so every day, even if sometimes the clouds obscured it.

I left the deck for the last time, and went back inside to have my breakfast.

I would need it.

It was going to be a long hot day, although I hoped most of it would be spent in air conditioning.

Although that could not be guaranteed.

I remember one long train journey back from North Carolina years ago, where the air conditioning had broken down somewhere in Florida.

With a reliance on technology, the windows barely opened and we all emerged in Grand Central Station like drowned rats.

Except it was not water running from us.

The red tape was not too tangled in the new Brooklyn docks - although the new eye recognition proved faulty and caused a bit of a blockage.

Penn Station, by the time I reached there, was heaving, but organised - apart from the escalators.

There appeared to be no functioning lifts - sorry elevators.

The attendant seemed to have all the care and charm of an

airport baggage handler - shoving people onto the moving stairway.

On the other hand when we arrived at the waiting train: the Amtrak staff were a welcome relief.

Helpful and humorous: a great combination which made the almost ten hour trip not only bearable, but entertaining.

Furthermore the ample seat 'leg room' allowed for a comfortable nap.

Which it probably should since it was the cheaper night time alternative to a sleeping compartment.

And, best of all, the air conditioning worked.

So the time passed, as I watched the countryside do the same.

Each stop brought forth our guard who advised us of our progress - and rights.

"Washington D.C. capital of the country - if you want to smoke you may step off here - this is a stretch/smoke stop."

To which announcement there seemed to be a general exodus.

I later learnt this had been the first smoking stop since Boston.

Unless you chose to negotiate the escalators and brave their keeper, in order to reach New York daylight.

Later, just after the train left Richmond to cross the border into North Carolina, our conductor began distributing pillows!

With the explanation: "I have not done so before, because you will lose them and then ask for more."

I wasn't quite sure if this was a serious remark - and, if so, what the heck people were doing with the lost cushions.

We reached my destination just before 9pm - right on schedule - where we were advised "Raleigh, North Carolina - capital of the state. If you want to smoke you may step off here: this is a stretch/smoke stop."

In a way I was a little sorry to say goodbye.

My sister was waiting for me.

Usually people opt for business before pleasure, but in this case I had decided I could combine the two.

So began the last part of my journey, and with it the last part of this narrative.

But not quite yet.

We stopped off at a Mexican eatery, where we joined my sister's children and grandchildren.

It was almost midnight before we arrived home.

My sister and brother-in-law's detached wooden single storey house in the countryside outside Clayton.

Fortunately she had to be up early for work at a local school, so any 'catch up' gossip could wait until tomorrow.

I knew my way to the spare room: I had used it before.

I remembered a previous warning about my sister's cat 'black socks' who would regard anything left on the floor as a potential litter box.

So I closed the door - making sure she was on the other side - before opening my suitcase.

I just had the time and energy to undress, before I collapsed onto the bed.

The next few days were hectic after the peace and quiet of the ship.

My brother came up from his home in Florida to pay a visit and take me to breakfast at the local Cracker Barrel.

A chain of country stores incorporating a restaurant with actual waitress service.

The smells from both were intoxicating.

The store itself was full of spiced scents, predominated by cinnamon.

The restaurant - not to be outdone - was the only place I knew which served a proper meat and two veg menu.

Which made a nice homely change from the usual aromas associated with fast food cooking.

But I digress - again!!

My sister was working most of the first week I was there, so I was left pretty much to my own devices - which suited me perfectly.

I had some research to do, but before I did anything else I needed to get some transport.

I knew where Craig lived - not far away - in fact next door in American terms.

But in American terms you cannot get anywhere without a

vehicle.

Unless you live in one of the cities where public transport is more widely available.

Even walking more than a few yards is not an option.

Not in the South at this time of year.

If the heat doesn't get you, the humidity will.

It would be suicidal act of stupidity for an alien like me.

So driving licence and passport in hand , before my brother returned to his family in Florida, I asked him to take me to the nearest Hertz - or equivalent.

I picked a small 'compact' car - it was all I would need.

The salesman joked it would be fine for my requirements: unless I was planning on transporting a body!

I think, for some reason, one more saying came to my mind: 'many a true word.'

I hope it wasn't prophetic.

The next day, after my brother and sister left, I checked out the car's GPS system.

An extra I never much bother with at home.

I fall into the 'back to basics' category when it comes to negotiating my way around.

A paper map is fine for me.

It is something I understand and trust.

Following an unfortunate incident a few years ago, when blindly following instructions would literally have led me to my final destination!

Besides, by now you may have realised I do not like relinquishing control.

Particularly to a disembodied voice, even if it sounds like Arnold Schwarzenegger.

In fact, especially if it sounds like Arnold Schwarzenegger!

But in this instance I had no choice.

So after lunch I keyed in the zip code and set off.

It was intended as nothing more than an initial recce.

But in fact it told me much more than I knew.

Much more than I wanted to know about Mr Craig Wurley.

It told me, what I suppose I always knew, at best he was a

criminal, at worst a murderer.

He may be many things, but he wasn't a serial killer.

Everything he did was motivated by greed and power.

Not in itself a crime.

In fact many prominent people have reached their positions by the single minded pursuit of both.

Many are congratulated, and even rewarded, for their self centred ambitions.

But, as far as I was concerned, Craig was guilty as charged.

The trial was over.

# Chapter Thirty:  Retribution


So I have reached the verdict.

At the accusation of putting the cart before the horse, now let me give you the evidence.

That day, when I visited the neighbourhood at the end of my GPS directions, I was prepared for many things, but not what I found.

A beautiful two storey southern mansion worthy of a set from 'Gone With The Wind.'

One thing was for sure, I would not be knocking on this door asking for charity donations.

So what was my best option?

Well I knew I had one asset.

Most Americans find the English accent fascinating.

Although it is shared with many movie villains, generally it invokes a sense of trust.

So I felt I could safely find the nearest public building - like a store  or restaurant and ask some questions.

But, as luck would have it, I didn't need to.

I was sitting in my car just considering this approach, when an elderly lady walking her tiny dog approached me.

First of all she seemed a little wary, but started to relax when she saw me, and began to smile when she heard me speak.

"Oh how charming - you're English aren't you?"

A good start, because not many Americans can differentiate between accents in the English language.

The classic error, and one I have experienced, being mistaken for an Australian on a couple of occasions.

And when it comes to hearing the difference between English dialects, I know I am more likely to be mistaken for Made in Chelsea than Geordie Shore.

With my broad country accent I cannot understand this, but I understand why.

I love the diversity of every regional accent - but admit, even I have difficulty understanding some of those with more region and less recognised English.

But in this case the confusion worked to my advantage.

Once again I had found another new friend.

She asked if I was here to visit Mrs Wurley?

I said 'yes' - what was the worst that could happen?

I suddenly remembered asking such a question before in respect of Craig.

But this time I had a much more plausible explanation.

With my family living locally, it was perfectly natural I should look up an old friend and her daughter.

The woman continued to say she was sorry, but hadn't I heard - Mrs Wurley had died a few months ago.

The victim of a hit and run driver.

I was shocked, but managed to ask about her mother.

At first this brought no recognition, but then she remembered.

There had been another, older, English woman, a long time ago, who had come for a visit.

Then she disappeared.

It was assumed she had gone back home.

From what I could gather there was not much contact between the neighbours.

The women were friendly enough as passing acquaintances.

But it was obvious Mr Wurley was not a very sociable character and discouraged the tendency in others.

Therefore she knew very little about him, including his job, although he seemed to spend a lot of time away.

In fact he was away at the moment.

Fortunately her little dog was becoming hot and bothered by the heat, so we said our goodbyes and I left.

There was nothing more I could do here, and I needed my laptop.

The rest of the day, before my sister returned, I spent searching the local news, beginning with Debbie's death.

Not much there and no mention of any relatives - except a mother living in England.

Who I suspected was no longer living anywhere and whose present whereabouts was much closer.

Finally, as I have said many, many times before I don't believe in coincidence.

Odd then that Emma lost personal contact shortly after Brenda's arrival in America, and that she fell completely silent at the same time her daughter died.

So I found myself with a dilemma.

Do I go to the police with my suspicions, and there were plenty.

Debbie's death they had obviously investigated.

But Craig would have made sure to provide himself with a good alibi.

Probably away on one of his 'business' trips - whatever that entailed.

Certainly plenty of witnesses.

Besides, knowing Craig, he wouldn't get his own perfectly manicured hands dirty.

So that would be a dead end.

No one likes to admit they have made a mistake, least of all the authorities.

But if you add to this the earlier disappearance of the mother, then there may be a case for a closer look.

An examination which may delve into Craig's life, and wonder how he could afford the lifestyle he now enjoyed.

An extremely extravagant one if the house was anything to go by.

They would check up on his finances.

Because he either had a very well paid job, or another source of income.

Knowing Craig it would not be a purely legitimate one.

It may not stand up to a closer scrutiny.

I could also point them in another direction.

One which led to the whereabouts of Brenda's bank account, which would have been considerable.

Since it included the income from the sale of her home in Bath.

There was yet a further avenue to search.

Before Debbie had left her mother told me her concerns about Craig's motives.

Her daughter would shortly be the recipient of a very substantial endowment left to her by her father.

I had one worry in all this speculation.

Surely Debbie had not been party to all of this.

She may have become an accomplished liar, but the idea of her complicity in fraud and murder, was unthinkable.

No I didn't believe it

What I could believe: there may have been an argument between mother and daughter.

Probably engineered by the son-in-law/husband.

Once Brenda left the scene Debbie was easily convinced that she had returned home.

Particularly when she later received apologetic and loving emails.

I had no doubt whatsoever who was the author behind those messages.

If Craig had so successfully passed himself off as Brenda to Emma then he could have done the same to Debbie.

He could easily concoct some correspondence allegedly from Brenda, and at the same time intercept cards and emails sent from Emma.

It was a juggling act, but he had a lot of experience.

And Craig had a major advantage - love is blind.

But perhaps with age and experience Debbie had finally opened her eyes.

Or had them opened for her.

Maybe she had found out something which made her life more of a threat than her death.

I was increasingly more and more certain the hit and run was no accident.

So what do I do?

I am a stranger in a strange land.

A land which may share the same language - well basically - but culturally, and legally, is very different.

I dare not get involved in any form of vigilante justice here.

If I did then I may very well find myself on the wrong side of the window in the execution chamber.

Although in fact this was the one thing which tipped the balance for me.

In North Carolina they have the death penalty.

Not a solution I normally advocate.

But, if all my suspicions proved to be true, I would happily administer the injection myself.

So the next day I would make another journey - to the nearest police station.

Having made up my mind I spent a nostalgic evening with my sister, looking over old photographs and slides.

We shared a good laugh when we saw the fashions from the 1970s.

Enormous flared trousers which would have looked garish on a circus tent.

Yet seemed to have been so popular in the era they were shared between my mother and sister.

My brother seemed to be the only one who retained any sort of dress sense, limiting his colour range to brown, beige, orange, and just occasionally pink!

Sometimes all at the same time.

Thank goodness I was usually the photographer, so I featured rarely.

We went to bed early: tomorrow was sister's last day before a week's break.

I slept well, I like to think, the sleep of the just.

When I woke up my sister had already left.

Not unusual, but I must have been sleeping so soundly I hadn't heard a thing.

Anyway I hadn't told her about my plans, or in fact anything about the 'business' part of my visit.

I wouldn't be long.

It was only going to be a brief visit.

Just enough to set them on Craig's trail.

I had an early lunch, or brunch as they call it, and then left for the small local police precinct.

As soon as I walked into the front desk I saw a familiar face.

She time she was minus her dog, and I hoped she hadn't lost it.
Before I could speak, or even smile, she jumped up and
approached, not me, but the duty officer.
She began proclaiming in a much stronger Southern accent than
I remembered.
"That's her."
The result of excitement, because she continued.
"I saw her watching the house yesterday."
Everything then happened so quickly.
She was restrained and placed back on her seat, reserved for
complainants - the innocent.
I was ushered into an interview room, the first link in a chain of
custody for criminals - the guilty.
At that moment I realised I was a suspect.
It didn't take long for me to understand why.
Apparently Craig had been found dead at his luxurious home
this morning.
Not only dead, but murdered.
Someone who was either a very good shot, or very close, since
the bullet had gone through the centre of his forehead.
I had come here prepared to be a witness for the prosecution,
but I quickly envisaged myself being put in the dock.
At first I hoped this would be quickly resolved and I would walk
out of here within minutes.
In my head I went over my defence.
How and where did I get a gun.
Hardly a method of choice for a middle aged English woman!
And why?
Craig's guilt - if proved accurate!
Although I already knew any evidence against him, would now
provide my motive.
As would my accent: I was a foreigner, or in the less than
pleasant words of immigration: an alien.
In which case the 'charming' English accent may now work
against me.
Overnight I had become the 'bad guy' film stereotype.
If the details of Craig's life became public, many may

sympathise with my feelings and motives,  but the justice system
would grind onwards.
Perhaps for years.
I may avoid execution,  but a life sentence it may prove to be
infinitely worse than a death sentence.
I could end my days in a maximum security prison, surrounded
by the worst of the worse,  thousands of miles away from home,
with no hope of reprieve.
Within a very short time the interviews were over.
I barely remember the questions,  let alone my answers.
When we finished,  I was escorted,  not back to the front office,
but into the cells where I still remained.

Although apparently it is only an urban myth about one 'phone
call.
In fact detainees may be allowed several, or none,  depending on
the severity of the crime.
In my case it was probably the highest,  but nevertheless  I was
allowed one.
I only needed one - to my sister,  who else did I know?

# Epilogue

She, in turn, makes one 'phone call, to the only person she thinks may be of use.

The husband of an old friend: an ex highway patrol officer.

Someone in a position to ask questions and, more importantly, obtain the answers.

It is he who, at the eleventh hour, well actually the seventy second, comes to visit me and brings my pardon.

Well not exactly, but the answer to many questions which will set me free.

He explains, briefly now, but in detail later.

It turns out the house was not a legacy from Brenda or her daughter, but other unfortunate relatives, who died some years earlier.

His parents, who were victims of another hit and run.

Not a very original person - our Craig.

The authorities even managed to trace the man he paid to run the old couple down, who had turned state's evidence for a plea bargain.

A man from his contacts in the drugs industry.

Something he had become involved with in order to sustain his lifestyle.

A 'profession' which contains some very unpleasant and dangerous people.

People for whom firearms were a way of life, and the perfect solution to a problem.

Which Craig threatened to become, once a spotlight was shed on his extra curriculum activities.

So the police had a much more likely suspect than myself.

I was allowed to go.

No bail, no apologies.

Except for my friend.

Officer Williams, who warmly shakes my hand, and hopes I do not judge them too harshly.

As we exchange our goodbyes, now as equals, I am aware of a

new inmate passing us.

A young fragile looking girl.

She will be in my cell tonight, but I don't feel any sympathy.

I do feel something else.

Something which makes me grip Officer William's hand tighter and whisper: "don't trust her."

He looks at me, but doesn't say a word.

But within two days I will hear from him again.

He rings to let me know, before I hear the news.

There has been a terrible incident at the gaol.

No one knows how it happened, but despite his warnings, one of the wardens is dead.

Somehow the girl obtained a knife and cut his colleague's throat.

It would not be the last time I heard from him.

## Books published by same author

Circles ( biography) 2012    : life in Temple Cowley from
                                         1905 - 1993

The Executioner's Tale 2014  : thriller/detective story

 I Am Not There  2015     : biographical/supernatural

A Cure For All Ills  2019    : sci fi/man made pandemic


**Self publishing website:  www.ginnystroud.com**

Printed in Great Britain
by Amazon